Flying Saucers
A science fiction novel

Richard G. Hole

Science Fiction and Fantasy

SYNOPSIS

Slowly, the so-called Flying Saucers were becoming more topical. For it was not the fleeting vision of any uneducated peasant who had thought he saw a strange flying object on his farm. Men of recognized solvency and good judgment also claimed to have seen them. Above all, in the southern part of the American continent, specifically in Argentina, Chile and Brazil.

From here, astronomers, physicists and many men of science, put aside their particular experiences on fleeting visions, and even photographs that had been obtained of the Flying Saucers ...

Flying saucers is a story belonging to the Science Fiction series, a collection of science fiction and fantasy novels

FLYING SAUCERS

CHAPTER I

It is an obvious truth, but it must be constantly remembered: the Earth is not alone in the Universe.

Everything at most is a tiny point in Infinity, where the eternal lights of the stars trace their dance steps. In that tireless dance they gather in the Spirals, in the Globular Conglomerates and in the countless Milky Ways.

All this forms the Cosmos: the Universe.

Each Milky Way is a large family of stars, where some billions of stars are grouped. Each star is a sun and, in turn, each sun has its planets as children.

Each planet can be an Earth-like world. Its possible cosmic inhabitants can be in a thousand ways or be constituted in a thousand ways, according to their own setting: with their peculiar characteristics.

Arriving here, the imagination wears out.

Man knows all this, at least he senses its existence. But he is lost in the Hereafter and is terrified, so he adopts the naive policy of the ostrich, hiding his ignorance in Olympic oblivion, if not, absurdly denying all these possibilities.

But it is an oblivion from which, periodically, it has to come out due to the course of events. As of 1945, these events began to happen, first, gradually and then, little by little, in stages, but with greater continuity; On the Earth, here and there and apparently in a capricious way, strange flying objects began to be seen, which the journalists called Flying Saucers, perhaps due to their spherical shape.

The Second World War had recently ended, and the dates also coincided with the appearance of the first jet flights. Modern airplanes flew at supersonic speeds and, generally, poorly informed, people believed that they were new experimental flights, carried out by some of the great powers.

However, slowly, the so-called Flying Saucers were becoming more topical. For it was not the fleeting vision of any uneducated peasant who had thought he saw a strange flying object on his farm. Men of recognized solvency and good judgment also claimed to have seen them. Above all, in the southern part of the American continent, specifically in Argentina, Chile and Brazil.

From here, astronomers, physicists and many men of science, put aside their particular experiences on fleeting visions, and even photographs that had been obtained of the Flying Saucers. The tabloid press echoed such stories and it can be said that they made a killing. There was a columnist who began to write about the possibility that the Martians wanted to visit us, making their first contacts on those flights.

All this raised a formidable controversy and for some months nothing else was discussed. Many had fun, others speculated, and very few took it seriously. Most of them trembled inwardly, no matter how much they said so as not to pass for cowardly or fearful.

But the question still stood. Did Flying Saucers Really Exist?

It was up to the authorities of the great powers to decide on the case, but, illogical as it may seem, they did not. They limited themselves to communicating that none of them carried out flight experiments, which were not already known and also practiced by other countries. Consequently, they had nothing to do with that fantasy of the Flying Saucers, which could well be mere illusions of the ignorant, or phenomena when observing the atmosphere.

However, as the mirages multiplied more and more, the Flying Saucers continued to be talked about. Soon there were thousands of people willing to claim that they had seen the strange flying objects. Even the occasional clever or studious person comes out who, compiling all the incoherent stories, published books on the case. Volumes that were sold in careful editions and that became the most discussed and commented best-sellers of their time.

However, the interest of the people began to decrease around the year 1965, since the Martians did not decide to land on Earth. Twenty years is a long time, for people to keep their attention on the same thing, especially when daily living demands to put it on more tangible and more concrete things.

And that, during those twenty years, the Flying Saucers did not stop making their periodic appearances in many places. Even at the Parisian airport of Orly, on a certain day in June 1960, for five long hours the flights in and out of the French capital had to be interrupted, because, without possible explanation, several unidentified flying objects remained high above the airport.

As if they were watching him!

They arrived unexpectedly and left in the same way, five hours later. Around that time, another no less curious and surprising case had also occurred. A British BEA pilot, when commanding his large jet packed with passengers, saw orange and blue beams of light in front of the aircraft, which, at first, he took as refractions from the Sun. But he soon had to change his mind, when his The copilot indicated that a silver-colored spherical ship was flying ahead of them, at high speed, and without making any signal.

Alarmed, the same passengers were able to see the strange flying object that, capriciously, despite carrying the double supersonic speed jet, in a single second disappeared from their sight, ascending into the sky.

The case of the North American pilot Perry Lhomar was also registered, the day that flying over Fort Knox on his watch over the United States Treasury, he communicated by radio to the base that something strange and unknown was flying over the place where more gold is stored. in the world. That pilot asked permission to chase the flying object and, bravely, Perry Lhomar ascended with his very fast X-15 without being able to reach it.

It simply disintegrated in midair, reaching a height and speed prohibitive for the endurance of its X-15.

Then a few months later, everything else came ...

The version that some Martians had landed on a plain in Mexico. That of some charred crops in a certain place in Australia, with all the signs that some spacecraft had landed there. And, scattered among other news also about Flying Saucers, the confusing statement of a certain Ralph Mayer who claimed to have spoken with two strange characters barely a meter in height, after having seen them descend from his Flying Saucer in the cold mountains of the Highlands, north of Scotland.

By this time, a man had already been put into orbit on Earth and the Russian Gagarin belonged to the history of the pioneering astronauts. The experiences in this order soon multiplied in the following years and none of the astronauts could claim to have encountered other space travelers.

However, in the face of thousands of cases without a possible explanation, an international body was created, which decided to adopt the acronym UFO, to collect all the data and thoroughly study everything that refers to Unidentified Flying Objects.

Those responsible for UFO ordered to carry out deep investigations, carried out with so much secrecy that, twenty years later, already around 1985, nobody could assure, in a serious discussion, if the Flying Saucers were a reality or, simply, everything was pure fantasy.

In a word: everything was the same as in 1945, when forty years ago some inhabitants of the Earth raised the first alarm bells, assuring that they had seen unidentified flying objects.

Well, nobody could assure you that UFOs did not exist, except some of the high heads of that International Organization ...

But, between them, they justified their silence, so that the inhabitants of the Earth would not be alarmed, creating a true cataclysm.

Yes, it was true that the Earth was being visited by strangers to the Planet. And the most surprising thing was that those visits did not go back only to the last twenty or forty years. The researchers worked well, and the report they presented to a small group of people was conclusive.

Apparently, and according to an in-depth study of all the data, the Unidentified Flying Objects had been making their periodic visits to Earth for ... MORE THAN EIGHT THOUSAND YEARS!

This surprising conclusion was reached after studying and analyzing the ancient texts of old civilizations, already lost in the long night of time. In China, five thousand years before Jesus Christ, there were already vague references to certain Flying Chariots that soared through the sky at great speed. These references coincided with those of the ancient Vedas of India, which, in turn, cited such phenomena in their holy books, written in the Sanskrit language.

In the same Bible, leafing through it and studying it carefully, references could also be found in this sense, which could later be staggered with the texts of the Egyptian scribes, when they made their compositions by order of the powerful pharaohs.

Later, already in the times of the fertile Greek civilizations, in many epic and religious poems, there were again, symbolically, references to Flying Chariots that passed over men, as they believed then, led by all that bunch of little Greek goddesses, of which their mythology is so full. The same chariot pulled by the spirited horse Pegasus, soaring in the sky, could it not have come out of the vision of a UFO?

The march of the capricious Mercury, ascending on his speeding chariot to Mount Olympus, did it not also mean the fleeting vision on the part of those imaginative people, of some Flying Saucer?

And, already in the Middle Ages, the vague references to such phenomena multiplied, although each writer and each country adopting its own particular way of interpreting them; balls of fire rising and falling from the sky; Meteorites that were descending at high speed announcing the end of the world, which never came, because, simply and inexplicably, when it seemed that they were going to collide with the Earth, they rose again to lose themselves in the infinite paths of the Cosmos.

More Flying Chariots appeared in medieval literature in great profusion of writings, they continued to be cited through the centuries. Until as early as 1945, when the men came out of their horrendous World War II, they began to bravely write about the possibility of the Martian visit.

All that made no sense, if you were not looking for a common motive: Flying Saucers or Unidentified Flying Objects.

There were the UFOs, the mysterious extraterrestrial objects that was a reality.

Of course, where did they come from? What corner of the Universe did they come from? What were your crew like? What were your intentions? Why had they been watching the Earth for so many thousands of years? Why weren't they openly seen? Did they want to invade it, or would they limit themselves to dominating its inhabitants, by terror of the higher, of the unknown?

There were so many questions to answer, so many suggestions raised about the problem, that in order not to create confusion and terror it was necessary to continue to jealously hide the secret of confirmation. The official centers continued to give evasions or more or less scientific explanations; the point was not to state the whole truth.

It was necessary to prevent mass hysteria from taking over the inhabitants of Earth. The great mass could solve nothing with its opinions and it did aggravate the situation even more, if it reacted in terror. The decisions corresponded to the Central Galactic

Government and, even within the International Organization that studied the case of UFOs, many members were not aware of what was happening.

First of all, once the existence of the Unidentified Flying Objects had been confirmed, what was convenient to know was what were the intentions of those mysterious extraterrestrial visitors.

And that, I was yet to find out ...

CHAPTER II

The high heads of the Central Galactic Government counted, to continue hiding their secret, with the particular inclination of man.

They knew that, at the most, periodically coming out of the lethargy of their boredom, their monotonous living and their meanness, their problems, the inhabitants of the Earth look up to the sky and question the Universe, trying to delve into its mysteries.

But when they do, the common inhabitants of the Earth get more fear than curiosity, more suspicion than scientific eagerness and also, why not say it?, More desire that for them everything remains the same and nobody comes to tell them that in Those bright spots that you can discover with the naked eye, in those stars, in those remote solar systems and in these galaxies, other rational beings may exist.

That is something that usually displeases them and many times they make fun of such a possibility, because it implies that there, in any remote corner of the Universe, any extraterrestrial race, any fantastic supercivilization, may exist and decide to come and visit us.

The average man dislikes all this. He has long believed that he is the King of Creation and the possibility that he is not, infuriates him. It also humiliates him, demeans him, and leaves him converted into a mere sample of the wonderful variety of Life.

The human race wants to remain the queen of the Universe and rejects, instinctively, and perhaps also arrogantly, all possible competition. His reaction is that of the spoiled child who sees the arrival of the new baby brother, a decrease in the affection of the parents.

Infantilism!

For this reason, man is not disposed, in general, to receive in a friendly manner the possible inhabitants of other worlds. On the contrary, he considers them in advance harmful, harmful and potential enemies, for him. Hence, he is eager to reject them, if they ever dare to approach his beloved world.

To a lesser extent and by way of example, this has been the internal conflict of the human races.

They have always rejected each other, even even tribes and peoples of the same race.

Remote antiquity tells us of the struggles between Assyrians and Babylonians. Between Egyptians and Hittites. Between Persians and Greeks. Between Romans and Barbarians. Between Carthaginians and Romans. Between Vikings and Normans. Between French and English. Between Spanish and indigenous peoples, when the American colonization.

For centuries, each race, each people, took up arms with the intimate conviction that they were right. And every battle won against the enemy was attributed to a gift from heaven.

To a divine grace.

And God, afflicted, but without intervening in these fratricidal struggles, continued to leave them to their free will, until they themselves, guided by their reason, ended up uniting in a common people and feeling that they were all children of mother Earth.

Yes, all children of the same planet, why not get to understand each other?

With the passage of time, man began to understand and his planet was pacified, constituting the Central Galactic Government. Being white or black, yellow or copper, was considered to be rather the geographical result than a reason for disagreement.

The other small differences were also bridged.

But now he would have to start over. Now he would possibly have to fight extraterrestrial beings.

Until he colonized other planets, other worlds and other galaxies, or until they enslaved him ...?

* * *

Faced with such a responsibility, the high heads of the Galactic Central Government met, the latest conclusions of those who took care of the study of UFOs demanded it.

And in his capacity as Secretary of Defense, Lieutenant General Paul Quiin proposed with his characteristic energy:

"Enough arguing, gentlemen! What we must do, we all know very well. Destroy those damn Flying Saucers!

There was a murmur throughout the room, and at last the slow voice of the atomic sage Curt Hartman inquired, with a slight smile:

"Very good, General Quiin. But ... do you want to tell us how?

Visibly upset, General Paul Quiin replied:

"That question is whimsical, Professor Hartman. We have weapons powerful enough to do it! And you know it!

"Are you referring to our atomic cannons, General?

Lately, everyone knew of the friendship between the energetic General Paul Quiin and the easygoing Professor Curt Hartman. That is why they were not surprised when the Secretary of Defense answered, with the same irony:

"Exactly, professor! I was referring to our atomic weapons in the manufacture of which, precisely, you have been involved so much.

"That is why I know that they will not be effective.

This time it was not General Quiin who answered, when the Secretary of Armaments Sean Buttons, who inquired, preceded him, as surprised as the rest of the assembled:

"Are you suggesting that our atomic weapons will be ineffective against those Flying Saucers, Professor Hartman?

"Assuming that, is as much as admitting that we are defenseless" said someone else.

" It's stupid! "Rejected another voice." Nothing can exist that can withstand an atomic explosion!

Professor Curt Hartman raised his manicured hands and pleaded, in his slow voice, as he looked at everyone:

"Easy, friends! I have not said that these spaceships are invulnerable to an atomic impact. I am a man of science and I know well that all matter, no matter how hard and resistant it may be, can be disintegrated ...

" Then...?

"I have limited myself to saying that it would not be effective. It is not the same!

" Why not? "General Quiin returned to the charge.

"Because ... What would we gain by destroying one, or twenty, of those ships, in the event that our atomic cannons could surprise them and hit them?

"Give them a good lesson! Indicate that we are not willing to allow them to walk quietly in our outer space! And much less, let them get close to Earth!

"Bah! They've been doing that for thousands of years, General Quiin. Or has he not read the UFO reports?

"I have read them! But I don't agree with that part. I refuse to believe that these Flying Saucers have been observing Earth for thousands of years.

"The report is very meticulous", pointed out, with some irony, Professor Hartman. In particular, I find it very successful.

"Ultimately, that matters little to us now" again the Secretary of Armaments, Sean Buttons intervened. What interests us are his latest conclusions. Knowing that UFOs are a reality!

"On the contrary, Mr. Buttons" Professor Hartman cut him off. " Knowing that they have been observing us for thousands of years is very important. A lot of!

" Because? The urgent thing is now! The certainty that now they do!

Professor Curt Hartman fixed his lively little lashless eyes on the Secretary of Armaments and said:

"You suffer an error of appreciation, dear friend. Many of you suffer from it, I see!

"Do you want to explain yourself, professor?

"With pleasure, Mr. Buttons ... With pleasure!

The calm of that man was exasperating. They were discussing such a vital and urgent question, and yet he seemed to take pleasure in prolonging their answers. The smile appeared on her thin lips again when she added:

"I repeat that the conclusions of the UFO are correct and that I take it for granted that these extraterrestrial beings have been observing us for thousands of years. This implies that, in remote times, they had an advanced technique capable of approaching our planet.

He paused, before continuing, after looking at everyone:

"Many things can be deduced from that, gentlemen... Many! And one of them is that they must also possess atomic weapons. Or even more powerful!

Silence reigned and, with a certain smile, he finished:

"Doesn't that make sense to you, gentlemen?

"Well, Professor Hartman... So what? "Said, at last, General Paul Quiin." If necessary, we will fight!

Professor Curt Hartman again turned to him, repeating:

" To struggle...? How and against whom?

"Against those Flying Saucers or those UFOs!

"Well, do you know if the crew of those ships are really our enemies?

"We also don't know if they are friends. But they are invading our space! That is symptom enough to seriously warn you.

"A clean shot, General Quiin?

"Why not, professor?

"For many reasons: one of them, because we don't know how they can respond. So far we have not bothered them and they have done nothing to us.

"Forget one thing, Professor Hartman; Until now, we were not sure that they were ships built outside of Earth.

Curt Hartman appeared to give up on the discussion, admitting:

" In agreement! All right, General Quiin! Let's be crazy enough to declare war on another extraterrestrial race, of which we know nothing, other than the certainty that they have a technique far more advanced than ours. Let's be crazy enough to launch the entire Earth into a possible cataclysm! And let us also be stupid enough to destroy what may be an attempt at friendly rapprochement by those beings who, surely, if they had wished, could destroy us long ago! Do you think?

The spiel of the elderly Professor Curt Hartman had the effect he desired on those assembled. And soon the voice of President Leo Proebe was heard when he admitted:

"Okay, Professor Hartman. What do you propose?

This time the calm professor did not delay his answer by exclaiming vehemently;

" Peace...! Understanding...! Understanding!

From an angle in the large chamber, someone asked;

"What if they don't want it that way, professor?

Turning his head sharply there, the questioned confirmed:

"They have already shown that they want it that way. I repeat that they would have already annihilated us, had they wanted to!

"You have excessive faith in these mysterious beings, Professor Hartman.

" Yes! Can you tell us why?

Professor Curt Hartman seemed to hesitate, reverting to his leisurely way of speaking, saying:

"No... I can't tell you why I have faith in them. At least, with solid and demonstrable arguments. But my faith is intuitive ... I'd say deductive, gentlemen!

"Why deductive?

"Take a moment to think a little and you will also deduce: beings who have reached a degree of perfection in the technique capable of traveling through the outer spaces, necessarily have to belong to a super-civilized people. And as far as I know, civilization is always improving, not brutalizing.

"Judging on supposed grounds, Professor Hartman" again spoke the energetic Secretary of Defense, Paul Quiin. That reasoning applies to the human race. But is it valid for them? These beings, whoever they are, do they react the same as we do? Do they have the same concepts about morality? The same ideas about right and wrong?

"You have to trust that this is the case, General Quiin.

What if we are wrong? And if we judge them with the same human measure, which is not theirs?

"We will have to take that risk.

" I disagree!

Again the discussion became heated and even violent and, who else who less, getting excited and getting up from his seat, exposed the same fears as General Paul Quiin, who again gained ground from Professor Curt Hartman. Instantly he realized that he and his supporters were being overwhelmed, so he began to shout:

"Crazy! You will lead the human race to collective suicide!

As the current President of the Galáxico Central Government, Leo Proebe demanded silence and announced:

"It will be put to a vote!

Broken his nerves, calculating that he would be defeated, Professor Hartman turned to the President and exploded:

"That is ridiculous, Mr. President! There are things that should not be put to the vote of the cretins!

His insulting words raised a new tumult with angry protests until the President replaced

"Please, Professor Hartman! Be more restrained. Each of the men gathered here deserves your respect,

"No, when they act like fools! The democratic voting system has more than once led to disaster. I laugh at the wit of the human race! It's gross!

And amid a clamor of protests, he left the meeting, muttering to himself under his breath:

"You morons! I will have to vary the plan ... They will force me to destroy them all!

Then, already on the street and calmer, he reflected again:

"I will consult it ...

CHAPTER III

Lise Borg engaged the autopilot and no longer worried about the vehicle.

The girl had complete security in the electronic system that regulated the intense traffic, by means of an endless number of photoelectric cells, which came into operation every time a driver switched on his autopilot. Thanks to the ingenious system, traffic accidents had been reduced to a minimum in the last hundred years. Practically, no vehicle could collide with another because the photoelectric cells acted effectively on the brakes, allowing the car that had the preference to pass without reducing speed.

Rollovers or distractions on the highways were also completely impossible; The magnetism of the track acted on the wheels in such a way that, even leaving the vehicle in total freedom of movement, it did not allow the car to leave it, unless the corresponding control did not act to be free of that magnetic force.

That security was the result of the technique and science that man had achieved to improve his constant development on the old planet he inhabited.

From the Department of Acoustics to the Prestwich Astrodrome, Lise Borg knew there were more than twelve hundred miles and with her blue eyes she gazed out at the landscape speeding past them. Very green meadows, very distant mountains with blue and brown tones and, from time to time, groups of trees that announced the proximity of a farm, a hamlet or some collective farm.

That quiet life, bucolic and peaceful, away from the constant hustle and bustle of the big city, where everyone seemed to be in a hurry and always having the seconds counted, as if they were going to die.

Like she did, Lise Borg.

Of course, when she was Captain Blay Farrell's wife, everything would change for her. He was stationed at the Prestwich Astrodrome and she would forever leave the noisy Acoustics Department in which she worked. There everything was noise, complicated devices to measure, control and know the intensity of these; oscillating displays that recorded in large graphs hertz, those units of frequency that are equivalent to one vibration or cycle per second

What did the sounds matter to her? Ever since he had known Captain Blay Farrell, he only showed interest in what his virile lips produced when he spoke words of love to him. An I Love You by Blay Farrell was worth the full range of sounds that could be recorded on his computer during his stunt career.

Although, to be honest with herself, Lise Borg had to admit that the haunting sensation of love had reached her precisely, through the study of sounds.

He remembered that day perfectly, he would never forget it. She was before her complicated computer registering the intensity of some vibrations, when a man's voice was behind her, saying:

"Hey, blonde, do you want to tell me why the hell they sent us this summons?

Lise Borg had turned angrily, to look at the inopportune visitor and yell at him to get out of her lab. But in the presence of that man, without knowing why, he stopped his impetus and could only remain with his mouth half open.

Like a silly schoolgirl!

When he recovered, he advanced toward the tall, broad-shouldered man in the uniform of a Space Forces captain. She felt watched by him from head to toe and she could also appreciate that he had unruly hair, brown and gray eyes, with piercing pupils.

Confused, she blushed at the admiring observation of the man, who showed the form in his hand, as she said:

"What summons are you referring to, Captain?

" This! I consider that it is not opportune!

Yes; Lise Borg remembered that meeting with Blay Farrell very well. And now, as she ran into his arms, she smiled, thinking it was only natural that she was so in love with him. That afternoon he was very arrogant and attractive, despite his anger at being summoned to the Acoustics Department,

She also remembered that at her exclamation, she could reproach:

"The only inopportune here is you, Captain! He shouldn't have entered this room, I was working and with his booming voice he has spoiled everything. The record of the sound I was analyzing ...

But he didn't let her finish and waving his brown-skinned hands, he cut off:

"To the point, blondie, I came in here because a girl told me that you were the boss. We want to know, Colonel Holtzman and I, what complaints you have against us. This paper says ...

"I know very well what that subpoena says, Captain! I signed it!

Then, he began to be more polite and correct, accepting:

"Well ... If only it had been an appointment to have dinner with you ...

"Not for dinner, Captain! It is to warn you that your jets do not make so much noise when flying over the city. They break down all our devices and, many times, we have to repeat the work.

"Look, blondie, Colonel Holtzman and I can order our men not to whistle or speak when they fly over the city. Understands? But ... Can you tell me how we can order the engines to make less noise, so that they don't disturb you?

"You will see a way to do it, Captain ...

"Farrell, blonde ... Blay Farrell.

"Thank you, Captain Farrell ... Well, as I said, you will see a way to avoid, that they pass over the Department of Acoustics.

"Do you want us to discuss that tonight, miss? I could come get her and while we have dinner ...

"I don't know if I should. Me...

"Ask yourself if you want what is better. I'll be here at seven!

Blay Farrell had turned on his heel and had no time to comment. But she had walked away because, since that happy afternoon, she had always done what he wanted. Deep down, wasn't satisfying him feeling happy herself?

Although now ...

Now he was doing something that Blay Farrell had forbidden him to do; approach the Prestwich Base.

Of course, Lise Borg justified herself by saying that a woman in love could not endure seven long weeks of separation. Colonel Alster Holtzman had ordered his pilots not to leave the Base under any circumstances and that was why she was going to visit the man she loved.

What could happen at the Base, so that Blay Farrell and the other pilots couldn't get out of it?

CHAPTER IV

Lieutenant Pat Summer tapped the king and the chip fell onto the chessboard, winning his partner Dickson Lolman. And to justify his defeat, he commented:

"Well, lucky in the game, miserable in love." You already know!

The jovial Dickson Lolman smiled too, rejecting:

"With you that doesn't go. You haven't kissed a girl in a century!

" Me? I have as many as I want.

"Now, now! That's why you begged Short's girlfriend to find you a friend, so the four of you could go out together. Here we find out everything, rascal.

"Of course, as in these weeks that we have been locked up here, there is no more to talk and gossip. Weasel!

The officer named Short protested, reminding his companions:

"What about patrol flights, Dickson?

"Don't complain, Short. Maybe there is little luck and we managed to intercept one of those Flying Saucers. You may bump into a beautiful Martian and ... I have been told that they are very pretty!

The laugh was general and one of the pilots added fuel to the fire:

"Pretty? Don't believe it, Dickson. They have told me they are horrible! With two horns on his forehead and a single eye ... Cross-eyed, to be exact!

They had to entertain themselves in something, in the seven weeks that they had been locked up in the Base. The order that the colonel had received from the Department of Defense was blunt: no one could leave the astrodrome under any circumstances. The patrol flights would be constant, both day and night.

The great Prestwich Base was in charge of monitoring all the airspace of the American continent, from Alaska and the Bering Strait, to Cape Horn and Antarctica, and at a height that was the maximum ceiling of modern reactors.

The spacecraft, which in number of fifteen were destined in the Base, would do the same service, but going back, due to their greater flight capacity, up to fifteen thousand kilometers, guarding outer space, with orders to shoot down any ship that was not identified by radio.

Of course, the Department of Defense had been forced to inform Colonel Alster Holtzman of the reasons for such surveillance measures. You couldn't send men to fight without at least telling them something about the kind of enemies they would have to face. In addressing such a problem the word Martian arose, although General Paul Quiin insisted that under no circumstances should the term be used, since there was absolute certainty about the mysterious Flying Saucers.

Specifically: All Air Bases on Earth had to monitor day and night, to intercept UFO flights.

They wanted to put an end to the espionage of the Unidentified Flying Objects. On the result of this vigilance, the life of all the inhabitants of the Earth could depend, who, at last, forgot their natural myopia, ready to face the great problem.

The crucial moment had arrived.

If it was true that for thousands of years they had wandered through space to monitor, and possibly destroy, the planet's defenses, now it was up to the inhabitants of Earth to surprise them in their persistent espionage.

Geologists claimed that the Earth had been spinning in space for billions and billions of years. In all that time, as long as an eternity, the Planet had gone through many vicissitudes, of all kinds. The vicissitudes of the last twenty thousand years had not been of a geological nature, but rather of internal conflicts, which its own inhabitants had created.

All that, at last, had been overcome. Peace reigned on Earth and the Galactic Central Government ruled the destinies of thirty billion beings who were no longer dedicated to exterminating each other.

But apparently a new cycle was beginning now. The cycle of the extraterrestrial fights, with cosmic beings, inhabitants of other planets that, possibly, watched the Earth from another Galaxy.

A gloomy panorama, full of unknowns.

But the pilots at Prestwich Base were young men, full of life and eager to give their own in defense of their planet. When they were given the surprising news, they had not been intimidated and rather were dedicated to joking with each other, before the moment of truth arrived.

* * *

A red light flickered across the panels of the Prestwich Base checkpoint. The sentry stepped up to the microphone to announce:

"Officer on duty! A vehicle is approaching on runway number six.

In the wardroom Lieutenant Dickson Lolman received the notice and replied:

"Okay, boy. If you don't turn onto the Cheviot Hills road, tell the driver that you can't go on. No one should enter or leave the Base!

"Well sir.

However, half an hour later the sentry had before him the blonde Lise Borg who asked him, in view of his refusal:

"Who is the officer of the watch?

"Lieutenant Dickson Lolman, miss. But I repeat that ...

"Tell him that Miss Lise Borg needs to speak to him.

The sentry looked again at the beautiful blonde girl, ending by admitting sulkily:

" In agreement! I haven't seen anyone more stubborn than you, miss.

A second later, he was communicating:

"Here's a blonde Venus who wishes to speak with you, Lieutenant Lolman. Insist on entering the Base! I already told you ...

Through the visophone, peering further into the screen, Lieutenant Dickson Lolman interrupted the sentry by repeating:

"A blonde Venus, boy?

All the other officers looked at him and he added:

"We already have them here! But instead of Martians, the sentry says she's Venusian and ...

The other officers smiled at his comment, though Pat Summer waved his hand in dismissal:

"Bah! You can keep it to yourself, Dickson. I give it to you!

More seriously, the officer of the watch faced the intercom screen:

"What the hell does that blonde want, boy?

"She says her name is Lise Borg and that she is Captain Blay Farrell's fiancée, sir. He arrived with his car like a rocket, ignoring the prohibitive signs and assures that he will not leave without talking to the captain.

"Lise Borg? Exclaimed the officer on duty.

And then, after a moment's hesitation, he announced:

"In twenty minutes I'll be there, boy. I'm going on the Grasshopper!

For all the personnel of the Prestwich Base a Grasshopper was the modern jet helicopters that, generally, were used to move from one part of the astrodrome to another. They also called the small two-seater airplanes, powered by atomic batteries, which had even greater speed, Stork.

Lieutenant Dickson Lolman adjusted his pilot's suit, requested the helmet from one of the orderlies, and announced to the other officers:

"Blay's girlfriend is here. I don't know what the hell I'm going to tell him!

"The truth, Dickson, who is on duty.

"And do you think it is normal that we have been in service for two months? Blay saw her, before, almost every day.

"Orders are orders, Dickson. No one should know that we are on the hunt for Flying Saucers!

The raspy voice of Colonel Alster Holtzman, confirmed, entering the great wardroom:

"Well said, Lieutenant Masson ... Our mission is a top military secret. Any distraction could mean collective panic, with very serious consequences.

They all squared their heads before the head of the Base, who added:

"I'll go with you, Lieutenant Dickson. I'll talk to Blay's girlfriend.

"Thank my Lord. She is a good friend and it would have been embarrassing for me to lie to her.

"We will have to do it, Lieutenant. Go!

Minutes later, covering the distance from the neuralgic control of the Base to runway number six, the jet helicopter descended to a hundred yards where the sentry was waiting with a nervous blonde girl.

Colonel Alster Holtzman saluted militarily, while Lieutenant Dickson Lolman offered his hand to the woman:

Hi, Lise. How around here?

"Very impatient, Dickson. What about Blay? I haven't seen him in a century!

The colonel intervened:

"Miss Borg... I'm afraid you won't be able to see Captain Farrell. And I suppose he told her she shouldn't come here.

"You told me, Colonel. But it's been about two months and I ...

"That doesn't matter, miss! Captain Farrell cannot leave the Base. Nor receive visitors!

Lise Borg had spoken to the man before, and she remembered that he had never been so abrupt and distant with her. He briefly crossed his blue pupils with the brown ones of young Lieutenant Dickson Lolman, to ask the question:

"What is it, colonel? There were never any inconveniences for family members to visit their pilots. I've been here many times and ...

"Everything is different now, miss. You must admit it like this and ask no more questions.

"It is impossible, colonel. Blay and I, we agreed to be married in three days!

"They will have to postpone the wedding... for now.

" Because? "Again he sought the eyes of the friend, when asking the lieutenant directly." Has something happened to Blay? Please, Dickson ... You must tell me!

Dickson Lolman was upset and only managed to say:

"Blay is fine, but we... The colonel will inform you.

Also annoyed by the commissioning of the officer, Alster Holtzman lied:

"Captain Farrell, as well as other of my officers, are... are. Arrested!

He saw the surprise and alarm in the girl's eyes and expanded:

"It is not of much importance ... Simple irregularities in the service. You will understand that we must impose discipline and ...

"Don't excuse yourself, Colonel. These are things I shouldn't get into. But I don't see the reason not to go in to greet Blay, once I'm here. However serious his fault may have been, I think ...

They had to stop when they heard the footsteps of the sentry running towards them from the control turret at the entrance, shouting:

"Colonel! Duty officer!

The energetic Alster Holtzman spun on his heel and, unperturbed, inquired, his eyes fixed on the soldier:

" What happen?

"It's from the Central Checkpoint, sir! You're getting messages from Captain Farrell's ship, Colonel! It's very urgent!

With alarm in her eyes, Lise Borg looked at the military man, who had lied, as she reminded him:

"Didn't you tell me that Blay was under arrest, Colonel? How is he piloting a ship?

There was no reply.

CHAPTER V

Colonel Alster Holtzman had not answered, being busy with the intercom, asking in turn:

"What is it, Major? Speak soon!

The voice came to them clearly informing:

"I put you with Captain Farrell, sir. Your ship has spotted a squadron of Flying Saucers ... And they're coming down on you!

Unable to avoid it, as if jolted by a spring, Lise Borg elbowed Lieutenant Dickson Lolman and the colonel away, rushing toward the microphone, calling:

"Blay! Blay! Can you hear me baby It's me! Lise!

* * *

About ten thousand miles above Earth, for the hundredth time in those three days of constant patrol, Captain Blay Farrell ordered his co-pilot:

"Plug in the radar screen, Claney.

Claney Hill glanced at the ship's commander, informing him:

"We're low on energy, Blay. That gossip is very consuming.

"What about the generator batteries, Sergeant Yay?

Sergeant Yay Banto, in turn, reported:

"We have had a breakdown, captain; a short circuit disabled them.

Blay Farrell looked at the dashboard panel, read some figures, and after doing a mental calculation, relayed to the ship's crew:

"We're back, guys. I already want to take a good bath!

Lieutenant Claney Hill looked at the atomic clocks and thought it appropriate to remind his boss:

"Our patrol doesn't end until 6.15, Blay. We still have three hours to go.

"I will tell the colonel that we have had a failure in the power generating batteries. Three more hours flying, and you'll tell me how we were going to land.

The radar screen had been turned on again, and at that instant Claney Hill leaned over to get a better look at the spot of light that was rapidly changing direction.

And her voice came out, alarmed:

"Look at this, Blay! That ship is upon us!

Blay Farrell did the math again, his pupils fixed on the pinpoint of light on the radar screen.

"It can't be Yoshi's ship or Ray's! Yoshi must be flying over the Pacific at the height of Hawaii.

He reacted swiftly and turned on the radio on the precise frequency wave, speaking excitedly:

"Yoshi? Here Eagle I to Eagle II ... I repeat: Eagle I to Eagle II ... Can you hear me, Yoshi?

Yoshi-Ito's voice, with his terrible English from being born in Japan, reached them, confirming:

"Eagle II to Eagle I. I hear you perfectly, Blay. What happens?

Calmer Captain Blay Farrell, asked:

"Are you following your normal flight route, Yoshi?

"Naturally, Blay. Why shouldn't he? Around here everything continues without news, although with each pass that we take to the Hawaiian Islands arouses the envy of my boys. We would like to go down for a swim on the golden beaches of Honolulu!

As they spoke, Blay Farrell's eyes kept staring at that eerie point of light on the radar screen, announcing to the commander of the ship era:

"Short, Yoshi ... I'm going to try to communicate with Ray.

Changed the wave frequency, bit by bit, Blay Farrell announced:

"Eagle I to Eagle III. Can you hear me, Ray?

This time the voice was nosy and Ray Stell reached them by reporting:

"Perfectly, Blay. We are low on now! For our clocks, two hours and forty-five minutes, to be relieved. Three days hanging out up here is pretty boring, guys.

"You go your normal route, right, Ray?

"What remedy? You and Yoshi have been luckier. How about the coasts of California and Canada?

"Wonderful, Ray! But there is something that I do not quite understand. On our screen we have a point of light that keeps getting closer. If it continues like this, in a few minutes we will have it on top ...

Ray Stell's throaty voice reached them, curdled with misgivings:

"A ... a point of light, you say, Blay?" Do you mean a spaceship?

"Yes, Ray ... I have also communicated with Yoshi and neither he nor you can be. From what I'm thinking it may be ...

"A Flying Saucer, Blay? Not!

"It is, Ray... and not one. There are several!

Blay Farrell cut communication with the Eagle III ship and searched for the frequency wave that would put him in contact with Prestwich Base. And when she finished transmitting the signals that identified her, she was able to inform the major of the Central Control Tower, no longer bothering to look at the radar screen:

"Major Loring ... Hold on tight, sir! We have five Flying Saucers, which are evolving to surround us!

Something like this was expected and, in those long seven weeks of constant patrolling, each crew had dreamed of being the first to discover the Unidentified Flying Objects.

However, it was one thing to dream of that encounter, and quite another to be in reality before the mysterious UFOs.

And apparently in a plan of attack, surrounding the ship commanded by Captain Blay Farrell. What would become of the Eagle

I, despite its powerful engines and the atomic arsenal with which it was equipped?

Major Loring accepted the advice of the captain who conveyed the message, clinging to the seat firmly, inquiring:

"Are you sure they're Flying Saucers?

The answer was overwhelming, without a doubt:

"They are, senior! Very large and shiny ships that seem to rotate on themselves, as on an invisible axis. They don't make noise and we don't know if they have motors or what energy drives them. But they are here, very close to us, throwing colored beams from their base, orange and blue, sometimes changing to green and deep red.

The information was completed by the voice of co-pilot Claney Hill, transmitting, in turn, to Prestwich Base:

"They don't seem to have windows, sir. They are metallic and I think hermetically sealed. At the speed they rotate, it cannot be observed well!

Major Loring was sweating profusely and unable to make decisions, relayed:

"Colonel Holtzman is not here! They tell me that he has gone to the control of track number six!

And then, as if forgetting something:

"Follow me, Blay! Do you think they are going to get close? If so ... Fire your atomic jets!

Blay Farrell, out of an instinct for self-preservation, and also thinking about the lives of the men who manned his ship, was about to actuate the controls that would set those deadly, disintegrating weapons in motion. No matter how supercivilized those beings who manned the Flying Saucers were, it was not presumable that they manufactured their ships with material capable of withstanding atomic disintegration.

But his thumbs went rigid, thinking of the enormous responsibility that, in those moments, fell on him.

If it disintegrated with one of the atomic jets, one of those five ships, what could come next on Earth? Those mysterious cosmic beings, would they not take a just revenge later on being attacked?

For an instant, he looked at the men in his crew. Lieutenant Claney Hill was too young to die. Sergeant Yay Banto had a wife and three children, and of the remaining five, two more were married men. Were they all going to die there?

Blay Farrell had the nagging feeling that every second that passed lasted a century. How many things could be thought of in a single fraction of a second!

Without knowing how, he found himself transmitting to Major Loring:

"Get in direct communication with the Colonel, Major Loring. Much depends on what we decide in the next few minutes, sir.

"I understand, Blay... I connect you to tower number six.

"Thank you, Major. And another thing, sir ... I am not going to fire the atomic jets, for now ...

"But...

"We will take our chances, watching them dance this dance around us. I reckon we could disintegrate two or three, but the others ...

"I understand, Blay. It is a prudent measure! I put you with Colonel Holtzman.

It was when, when entering direct communication with the tower on track number six, Blay Farrell heard the voice of the woman he loved, calling him:

"Blay! Blay! Can you hear me baby It's me! Lise! Talk to me please!

He was so puzzled that, for the moment, he could say nothing.

CHAPTER VI

He had to react, be calm and at last he was able to transmit, materially overturned on the microphone:

"Hi, Lise, sweetie! How are you there, at the Base?

But instantly, thinking that they had other things much more vital than themselves, in an urgent voice he asked:

"Look for Colonel Holtzman! It's very urgent, Lise!

Even his ship came the voice of the head of the Base:

"What is it, Captain Farrell? Major Loring told me ...

He hesitated for a moment in the presence of the woman, but he calculated that any objection was already late. Every second lost could be vital and that is why he ended up inquiring:

"Is that true, Blay?

"Yes, Colonel. They are Flying Saucers, UFO, or whatever you want to call them! But they are here! In front of us and surrounding us, sir!

"Shoot, Blay! Disintegrate them!

"There are five, my colonel!

"It's the same, boy! They have twelve atomic rockets! I order you to shoot!

Blay Farrell calculated the chances of victory; it was true that his ship had twelve atomic rockets, six attached to each side. But instantly he realized that he couldn't hit all five on the first volley.

In that dance around them, which seemed macabre to them, in their constant turning on an invisible axis, at least two of the five strange Flying Objects were located outside their angle of fire; the one who stood in front of them and the one who indicated on the radar screen that he was watching them from behind.

Suddenly Blay Farrell had to stop thinking.

Something seemed to explode in the earbuds she wore, threatening to make her lose her eardrums. After a series of clicks and confused noises, a voice with metallic bells made its way, ordering him:

"Follow us, Captain Blay.

Lieutenant Claney Hill touched his elbow, shouting:

"Our radio has been tampered with, Blay! They are the ones who have done it!

A series of deafening noises reached him again, before the same impersonal, metallic voice commanded again:

"Follow us, Captain Blay. Do not resist. They will no longer be able to communicate with Earth. Follow us, Captain Blay ... Follow us, Captain Blay ... Follow us, Captain Blay ...

The metallic voice did not stop. Unable to take that chorus any longer, Blay Farrell took off his helmet and headphones, trying to change the wave of the radio.

The helmet remained on the control panel and the metallic voice continued to emerge from the headphones, repeating tirelessly:

"Follow us, Captain Blay ... Follow us, Captain Blay ... Follow us, Captain Blay ...

The copilot followed suit, and Sergeant Yay Banto did the same behind him, the two of them also pulling off his helmet. But that was not why they were free of the imperious metallic voice, which continued without fatigue:

"Follow us, Captain Blay ... Follow us, Captain Blay ...

The commander of Eagle I looked at his crew, who were instantly all gathered in the central cockpit. Blay Farrell read bewilderment and dismay in their eyes, but not fear.

Not; fear had not yet made its appearance.

This reassured him, encouraging him to order them:

"Everyone to his place, boys. I'm not willing to follow those guys, even if they intercepted our communications!

"At the moment, they are the ones following us," Lieutenant Claney Hill commented.

It was true, Blay Farrell's ship continued to sail through space in the direction of Prestwich Base and the five flying objects, always circling them, were also following that direction. And apparently they did it without any difficulty, with no apparent strain on their engines, if they had them. They simply turned and turned vertiginously on themselves, at the same time that it also did it on Eagle I, speeding up or slowing down, depending on the ship that belonged to Earth did.

It was Corporal Doyer who asked the question:

"Are we going to shoot them, sir?

"Yes, Doyer... Let's shoot them! And we'll do it in a fraction of a second, when we're in the best shooting angle position. Okay guys?

"Yes captain...

Claney Hill was still hypnotized, looking at his helmet, listening to the metallic voice that did not stop ordering:

"Follow us, Captain Blay ... Follow us, Captain Blay ... Follow us, Captain Blay ...

"It's maddening! "Exclaimed the copilot." I would gladly send them to hell!

With a wry smile, Blay Farrell pointed at the radio.

"Give it a try, Claney... Maybe they'll listen to you and run away.

"Listen, you stupid! Can you hear me? Can't you say anything else? We are not going to follow you! You can go to hell!

New metallic, shrill noises screeched from the earphones, finally breaking through the same metallic, impersonal voice:

"They are wrong ... They are wrong ... They are wrong ... They are wrong ...

" Damn! They want to drive us crazy!

Claney Hill slapped his helmet furiously, and it rolled across the dash, tripping over the throttle lever. The engine nozzles entered another phase and the ship seemed to rebound in space, reaching full speed.

Thirty thousand kilometers per hour ...

When they managed to get up, Blay Farrell looked outside and everything remained the same. Apparently, the fact that they had doubled their speed did not affect their strange pursuers at all.

However, soon, the picture changed.

Twelve beams of yellowish light shot from the strange ship spinning before them, and as the tips of those beams struck the land ship, its crew members felt an electric shock.

Sergeant Yay Banto was unable to resist it and again rolled on the floor of the cabin, remaining next to the magnetized boots of his captain. Blay leaned over him:

"Okay, sergeant?

"Yes... yes, captain. I only lost my balance when I felt that jolt.

They helped him to his feet and he looked in all directions, questioning:

"Have you felt it too?

"Yes, sergeant. And I'm afraid the ship, too ... Look at that!

It was young Corporal Doyer who spoke, his index finger pointing to the dashboard, where a red light was constantly flashing.

"Failure in the oxygen reserve! The copilot yelled.

He could no longer doubt. The fight would be until the end and they had shown that they possessed electrical rays, with which they would try to destroy the land ship. But Blay Farrell calculated that much more powerful was the atomic energy that contained his Eagle I.

Twelve rockets that ...

"To your posts! "scream.

He went to remove his helmet on the dashboard when he realized that the irritating litany continued to come out of the headphones:

"They do wrong ... They do wrong ... They do wrong ...

Furious, Blay Farrell reached for the controls to maneuver, to make aiming easier. And he muttered through his teeth:

"Now you will see! I assure you that many of you will feel it! FIRE!

One of the strange flying objects ceased to exist, turning into an immense flare of all colors, as if the Rainbow itself had exploded. The space was filled with blazing explosions and the shock wave of that disintegration reached the terrestrial ship. Fleetingly, its crew members had the impression that the Sun had burst into a thousand pieces, disappearing a little from their sight, behind a gigantic cloud of smoke and vapors of all colors, always ascending, in the shape of a mushroom, upwards.

The dantesque spectacle was repeated, almost simultaneously three times to the right and left, in fractions of a second, and the voice of Corporal Doyer announced:

"Target rockets one, two, and three, captain!

"Good job, boy! "Congratulated, in turn, the commander of the ship." Let's go for the other two!

He turned the steering lever quickly, ninety degrees, so that in the dizzying revolt the remaining atomic rockets installed on the sides could head directly towards the other two enemies that were left to him.

But it was a useless work and too slow for the enormous speed of his two enemies who, faster than them, also varied the direction. Blay Farrell repeated the maneuver more quickly, and everything continued in the same way. A third attempt with the already frayed nerves, did not obtain better results.

" It's useless! "Protested." They beat us in speed and acceleration in maneuvers. We can never surprise them again to have those two within range!

For the first time in those agonizing minutes, young Lieutenant Claney Hill seemed to lose control of his nerves, and shouted:

"What can we do, Blay? Now they will strike us down on a whim, with their electric rays!

"Calm down, Claney, calm down ... When they haven't already done so, it will be for something.

It continued to descend and the contours of the Californian coast were already perfectly distinguishable with the naked eye. The sea and the land came out with great clarity and fleetingly, Blay Farrell thought that it was the same to be destroyed in one place than in another. Maybe better in the ocean, to save the trouble of identifying them.

Thinking about this, a name came to mind, Lise Borg, she had dreamed of marrying him and now ...

With a claw he caught the hull with the curious headphones where, impersonally, as if nothing had happened to the three strange companion ships of the other two that continued to pursue them, the metallic voice continued saying:

"They do wrong ... They do wrong ... They do wrong ...

"What are you waiting for, cowards? Get the hell out of us!

Before his screams on the radio, the litany changed for another that also emerged from the headphones:

"Keep descending ... Keep descending ... Keep descending ...

Blay Farrell stared at his co-pilot Claney Hill.

"It seems that they only change the song, every time we speak to them. Have you noticed, Claney?

" Yes! And it is very strange!

Behind him, the voice of Sergeant Yay Banto commented:

"Stranger is that, after they have seen what we have done with their companions, these two more, they do not attack us.

Blay Farrell came back on the radio.

" In agreement! Let's land ...

They only had to wait for the series of strident metallic noises to pass, to hear again the impersonal voice that was transmitting to them:

"We follow them ... We follow them ... We follow them ...

"How heavy! "We follow them, we follow them" "remedied Claney Hill." Why do they repeat things so much? They look like old parrots.

More sedate than his co-pilot, Blay Farrell headed the cave towards Prestwich Base, not without announcing on the radio, at least to change the monotonous tune:

"Why do you insist on following us? They'll catch you down there!

Following the metallic noises, the headphones said:

"We have a breakdown ... We have a breakdown ... We have a breakdown ....

Well; that was like breathing easy. They were closing in on Prestwich Base, judging by what they kept announcing now, it could be calculated that they weren't going to attack them with their electric bolts. It was all very strange and puzzling at the same time.

If the crew of those flying objects were beings from other planets, possibly from another Solar System, didn't they understand that if they continued to follow them and landed on Earth after them, they would be captured there? Did such an eventuality not matter in the least? Did they fear nothing? Were they totally devoid of feelings and for that reason they had not commented on the disintegration of the other three ships, their flight companions?

"All that scares me a lot," Claney Hill whispered softly. They may want to strike us down when we're on Base, so everyone can see their power. They want that on Earth they find out well ... They will take revenge!

Blay Farrell stared at his nervous young co-pilot and opined, showing nobility:

"Don't you think, deep down, they would have the right to do it, Claney?

"Why, Blay?

"You calculate, boy! We have no idea of the number of beings that manned those three ships that we have disintegrated.

"They asked for it! Let them stay in your world and don't come to bother us!

"We were about ten thousand miles from Earth when we found them, Claney. I do not know of any law that says that at that height the space belongs to our Planet.

"Monsergas, Blay! They wanted us to follow them. They repeated it a thousand times, like parrots!

The slow voice of Sergeant Yay Banto, again sounded behind the backs of the two friends, pointing:

"The strange thing is that they speak our language, Captain.

"Right, Sergeant! I already asked myself that same question. But I have given up answering it. All things considered, everything is very strange.

"Yes, my captain... there we have Prestwich!

"God grant the runways are clear and we can land. Without communication for a while, we have not been able to report what has happened, and that we return. And in good company!

CHAPTER VII

Despite the chase, Blay Farrell's maneuver was perfect and he put the Eagle I ship on runway number two, while the two Flying Saucers, spinning vertiginously on themselves, until giving the impression that they were not moving, did. at the end of runway number nine, at the extreme left of the Base, where there was no cement and the floor was parched and abandoned land, without any use.

From the lower part of those cylindrical ships, jets of steam of a thousand colors emerged that, despite the enormous power shown when lifting and calcining the earth, made little noise.

At last they were fixed on the ground, some five miles from the center of the Base, all in motion and agitated by the nervous coming and going of the men eager to each take their place.

The gunners lined up the atomic rocket cannons, toward the strange visitors. The other conventional weapons were also ready: twenty steel tanks, of enormous proportions, went into motion, leading the way to some fifty vehicles full of soldiers, also armed with bazookas and atomic rifles, which had only been tested in tests.

Twelve fire service vehicles raced there, thundering the air with the wail of their sirens, which made the atmosphere of agitation and alarm even more tense. Ten jets took off from the runways and began to evolve on the Base, in a constant vigilance on the strange artifacts that nobody could calculate what they contained inside their cylindrical bellies, about a hundred meters in diameter.

Megaphone in hand, on the platform of a speeding vehicle on track number two, where Blay Farrell's Eagle I was already perched, Colonel Alster Holtzman kept shouting orders in his deep bass voice:

"Everyone to your posts! May each one know how to fulfill their obligation! I don't want any failure, guys!

The loudspeakers also transmitted orders through the Base, while in the Central Control Tower, nervous and sweating profusely from every pore of his skin, Major Loring transmitted, in turn, those phenomenal news, directly to the Defense Department of the Central Galactic Government.

" Attention! Attention! This is the Prestwich Base! Two UFOs have landed on the Base! They are perched about five miles from center court! They have descended, chasing Captain Blay Farrell's ship! We are taking all the necessary measures!

Anyone who could hear the news understood that they were experiencing crucial moments for Earth. The history of man was going to change, from those moments, the human race was not alone in the Universe, as for millions and millions of years it was believed.

No one could be sure if this would be for the better ... or for the worse!

No one could guess anything.

Nothing at all!

The answer lay in those two huge surprise boxes, metallic and shiny in the sun, melted and manufactured in another Solar System, on another remote planet, on other worlds.

Feeling that was much more disturbing and, at the same time, intoxicating, than what Christopher Columbus and his audacious sailors could have felt when they discovered America.

Yes: it was much more so because it meant peering into one of the infinite windows of the Universe and coming into direct contact with beings strange to Earth. Authentic inhabitants of a New World, infinitely more interesting than the first Native Americans could have been, who were greeted by Europeans who crossed the great Atlantic Ocean for the first time.

The imagination was lost, bent on guessing and forming assumptions. It was useless to make an effort to conceive ideas or images that, possibly, in the face of reality, would have to be modified instantly.

One could only hope. And watch!

What were these mysterious beings like, and what did they want? Why, at last, had they decided to show themselves? What reasons did they have for doing this?

The unknown was still there, in those two Unidentified Flying Objects that, now, finally !, were going to be.

As they approached, Captain Blay Farrell briefed Colonel Alster Holtzman on everything that had happened. The head of the Base frowned and said only:

"Strange, Blay ... Very strange!

Lise Borg was materially glued to Blay on the platform of the vehicle, by linking the man she loved with one of her arms, around the waist, and allowing the pilot to pass hers over her shoulders. Busy with more important things that had been rushed, Colonel Holtzman had not found a way to forbid the girl from entering the Base. They had all had a terrible time when radio communications with Eagle I and the girl were cut off, she well deserved to be able to see, now, for herself, that Blay Farrell and his men had returned safely to Earth.

"I have had a terrible scare! "The girl whispered, hiding her face on the man's chest.

The hand now free of the glove, Blay Farrell pressed the feminine shoulder with affectionate movement, answering:

"Calm down, Lise. Nothing happened to us!

"But those ... those men who are in there, in those ships ...

The pilot smiled, to help reassure the woman:

" Men...? We don't know if they are men, honey.

"Worse still, Blay... If they turn out to be hideous and monstrous beings, I... I...

"You shouldn't have come, Lise. Colonel Holtzman shouldn't have let you ...

The aforementioned turned his head towards them, ceasing to observe the march of the vehicle towards the objective where they all converged.

"I couldn't help it, Blay. In any case, now you take care of your fiancée and stay away from those ... those ... artifacts.

Then he forgot about them to shout, over the megaphone, new orders:

"Form a circle! Let no one come closer than half a mile! The Shock Section on the front line! Set up the bazookas! The 5th and 6th Company, behind!

He left the megaphone in the hands of one of his assistants, to face the radio installed in the vehicle, entering into communication with the jets that flew over the area.

" Attention! Attention! This is Colonel Holtzman! Pay close attention to what I am going to say!

Before issuing the order, with the vehicle already stopped half a mile from the two gigantic extraterrestrial ships surrounded by vehicles and the twenty tanks full of soldiers, Colonel Holtzman glanced for a brief moment at the men who formed the Shock Companies and at the end, he added:

"In case of any emergency, if they see that the fight is established and we begin to bear the worst of it. Feel free to drop the bombs on the target!

Blay Farrell recognized the voice of Lieutenant Pat Summer, who was now commanding the jet squad. And his question had tones of anguish, when through the radio he inquired:

"The bombs, Colonel? Are you implying that ... we beat you guys too?

"That's what I said, Lieutenant Summer! If the fight starts and they start to beat us ... Raze this whole area! Is it clear?

"Yes, sir ... To order!

The pressure of Blay Farrell's hand increased on Lise Borg's shoulder. Their eyes met and silently the two understood the colonel's blunt order: if when the crew members of those ships left the fight began and, unfortunately, the terrestrial ones began to bear the worst of it, why hesitate to destroy them too , if with that measure it was possible to annihilate the strange visitors?

Paying the tribute of five or six hundred human lives in anticipation of what might come out of those two Flying Saucers was not a very high price.

In any case, the entire Humanity would remember their names, as heroes.

Yes: History would cite them as the first Earthlings who had started the cycle of the new struggle. The fight against the inhabitants of other planets. From other sidereal worlds.

It would be a pity if it happened like that, now that, at last, the Earth had managed to solve its internal problems and peace reigned throughout the planet.

Suddenly, Blay Farrell fixed his eyes on the radio set in the vehicle they were on. From there came metallic noises that he already believed he had heard, when he was flying over his ship. The driver was vainly trying to catch up with the wave that communicated with the jet squad. He did not succeed and only the presence of the strange Colonel Holtzman prevented him from releasing a refusal.

Blay Farrell calmed him down:

"Don't bother, boy. It's your interference!

"How, captain?

The dry question was asked by Colonel Holtzman, and the pilot tried to explain.

"Upstairs they also intercepted our radio. Either I'm wrong, or behind those noises we can hear a metallic voice that ...

Blay Farrell was not wrong. The car radio began to buzz:

"We have a breakdown ... We have a breakdown ... We have a breakdown ...

As he tirelessly continued the monotonous chant, this time, forgetting the woman's presence, it was Colonel Alster Holtzman who blurted out:

" Devils! Damned! They sneak around our planet and after intercepting our radio, all they can think of to announce is that they have a fault ...

He turned angrily to the radio and continued bellowing:

"Well, get out of here and we'll fix you up, hell!

Strangely, the song changed, repeating itself over and over again these words:

"Let's go out ... Let's go out ... Let's go out ...

Alster Holtzman turned to his officers and yelled, at the top of his lungs:

" Attention! All weapons ready!

Five hundred men fixed their anxious pupils on the two spherical ships. A thousand hands clenched their weapons, ready to fire. For a moment there seemed to be silence in all that remote area of the Prestwich Base, only torn by the air by the passes of the jets that flew at high altitude, also ready to intervene with their atomic bombs.

The noise that followed might have reminded Lise Borg of the faint hiss of her coffee pot, when she made her morning coffee, or when the pressure cooker announced that the food was ready.

But, a specialist in Acoustics after all, he identified the hiss as the pressure escape of some gate when it was activated, when it was opened. And suddenly, an intensely white beam of light struck his pupils.

CHAPTER VIII

The light came from a hatch that had been opened in one of the cosmic spaceships and would have blinded them if, little by little, as if by regulating its intensity, it had not been reduced to the normal one of a 100-watt bulb.

A folding metal ladder appeared through that lighted door and soon, impassive and rigid as automatons, the strange crewmen began to descend.

It was a unique moment, unparalleled, in the history of man, on Earth!

They were robots!

Yes, a dozen six-foot-tall, broad, massive robots with articulated limbs, laying the metal plates of their great feet on the steps of the ladder.

When they reached the ground, the rhythmic noise of their footsteps ceased and, always in single file, following the one who preceded them, they changed direction, marching rhythmically towards the concrete of the tracks.

It was an amazing and strange scene.

Mechanical beings!

Those were the inhabitants of other worlds?

Absurd: someone had to have created them, necessarily.

At last, the row of twelve robots, was stopped on the track number one and there the mechanical dolls turned around like disciplined soldiers. They remained rigid and immobile, as if the batteries or the energy that animated them had been exhausted. Only a blue flicker in one of the holes in their square, metallic humanoid heads announced that it was not.

Colonel Holtzman was finally able to shut the mouth that he had held open against his will. And he whispered in a low voice:

"Well, gentlemen ... Let's greet our visitors!

With one hand he stopped the movement of Lise Borg who was about to follow Captain Blay Farrell, ordering the blonde girl:

"No lady; now she will be a good girl and will remain here. Only the captain and my assistant will accompany me. Your presence could disturb them and... "he paused and wishing to make it all a joke, he continued." They must not be used to seeing such pretty women!

The courtesy and the energetic colonel's comments had that festive air because everything had turned out much better than they had originally expected. Fortunately, the first contacts with the strange visitors could not be more peaceful, and this is what made the head of the Base joke.

Lise Borg did not protest, and when the three men advanced a hundred yards, Blay Farrell opined:

"I think I should approach alone, Colonel.

"Why, Blay? Want to brag about the priority of this sensational encounter later?

"I'm serious, Colonel. They can be dangerous!

"I don't think so, Blay... Take a good look at them: they seem like perfectly disciplined soldiers. I wish my men would stand firm like this! It's nice to see you!

The three men continued to advance, managing to make out more details as they approached the twelve formed robots. Yes: they had two slits in the head for eyes and a lower one, as if it were the mouth. Throughout the ensemble you could see that whoever their builders were, they had tried hard to give them a human appearance.

It was thus denoted by those articulated arms and legs, with fingers on the hands, which could be capable of appropriate movements, to handle utensils. The body was solid, square like their heads, joined to the trunk by a spiral that should allow moving the upper part, to the right and to the left.

Blay Farrell calculated that, even though they were made of steel-aluminum, they might as well weigh a thousand kilos; it all depended on the complicated mechanism inside them.

With only a few yards to go, Blay Farrell deliberately took a few steps forward, leaving the colonel and his aide behind. And despite the new surprise, he could not help but smile when he observed that, surely moved by photoelectric cells that announced their proximity, the first robot that led the formation extended its metal arm, extending its hand.

The slit of his mouth flickered with blue tones and his metallic, cold and impersonal voice greeted:

"Hello how are you...? Hello how are you? Hello how are you?

Blay Farrell calculated that the litany would continue untiring, until he replied and with the waves of his voice cut that radio circuit, activated by the electronic brain that had been put to work when he approached. And that's why he answered, still smiling:

"Very good, friend. And you?

He was not mistaken: the repeated question of the first robot was replaced by other words, also tirelessly repeated:

"Damaged ... Damaged ... Damaged ...

Colonel Holtzman and his aide remained behind Blay Farrell, watching as the young pilot shook the robot's metal hand. And the head of the Base said:

"Let's save the introductions, Blay! This all seems ridiculous to me! An Army colonel saluting some metal dolls, God knows where they come from!

Blay Farrell turned to them, always smiling:

"They may be offended, Colonel! You have to be correct, don't you think?

"Correct? What a scare they have given us! Look at the one they have formed!

"We, sir, not them. Deep down, believe me I'm glad it's just about robots. That frees me from the conscience of having disintegrated three ships like those two.

Holtzman forgot the captain's comments, facing the first robot, who kept jumping his song:

"What about the other ship? Why doesn't it open?

"It is not necessary ... It is not necessary ... It is not necessary ...

"What is not necessary? "Roared the head of the Base." We need to know who's on it! If they don't come out too, we'll go in for them!

"They will do wrong ... They will do wrong ... They will do wrong.

"Noses! No robot, no matter how perfect, can tell me what I should and should not do on this Base. Is that clear, friend? And if I decide to have my men enter that artifact ... They will enter!

"It will be worse ... It will be worse ... It will be worse ...

" Wow! "Shouted the colonel." And above it threatens us!

The first robot began to formulate the repeated reply, when, instinctively, Blay Farrell must have interrupted its speaking circuit when addressing Colonel Holtzman:

"Please sir. I think we shouldn't get excited. So far, as surprising as it may be, everything is better than we thought. I ask your permission to try to clarify all this.

"All right, captain. Talk all you want with those stiff steel puppets! I am sincere when I say that it seems ridiculous to me to do so. The planet sending them must have been a little more considerate. A man cannot try to understand a machine!

"Why not, Colonel? If the machine reacts intelligently, man must not be less than it.

"Go ahead then, captain! They are all yours.

"Why not get them out of here? You can call cyber technicians to study the control of these machines. From its operation, from the form and materials with which they have been manufactured and from other tests, we can draw many consequences.

Alster Holtzman looked over the young captain's shoulder at the twelve outlandish robots in line, and said doubtfully:

"Well ... Now it is necessary for them to obey you and not refuse to follow you, Captain. But since they seem so friendly to you, go ahead!

Blay Farrell approached the first robot again, but wanted to experiment if the one next to him in line also had the ability to speak and directly asked him:

"Can you follow me? Nothing will happen to you. I think we have a lot to deal with ...

The answer came again from the first robot leading the formation, who even turned his head in the direction of the young pilot, answering:

"They don't speak ... They don't speak ... They don't speak ...

"It's okay. You answer me. Can you follow me?

"We follow you ... We follow you ... We follow you.

Blay Farrell turned smugly to the colonel and his aide, who was no less perplexed than the Base commander:

"Settled, Colonel. On going!

"On the move ... On the road ... On the move" the first robot began to repeat tirelessly, being followed by the other eleven.

But before the unusual parade that he saw passing before him, Colonel Alster Holtzman said to his aide:

"Tell the men to be vigilant.

"Well sir.

"It is possible that while they entertain us with those robots, the crew of the other ship will try to surprise us.

"Right, Colonel. They may be shipped as bait!

"I don't trust it at all! And I'm going to...

Colonel Alster Holtzman again was left with his mouth open, interrupting when the first robot said that as his circuit passed him, he caught his words:

"There is no deception ... There is no deception ... There is no deception.

The head of the Base could not help but exclaim:

" Amazing...!

CHAPTER IX

Old Professor Curt Hartman ordered, his voice slow but now angry:

"You have to kill them all! Those assholes know too much!

One of the men before him dared to point out:

"Sorry teacher. But that would raise suspicions.

"If things are done well, there will be no suspicions. It must look like an accident!

"It is that ... Five people and with such high positions, professor ...

"I will see that they meet at the Secretary of Defense's estate. Colonel Holtzman and Captain Farrell will not hesitate to attend the appointment of the idiot General Paul Quiin. After all, the two are under his direct orders.

"And Miss Lise Borg, Professor?

"He will also come. You will receive a message from your dear boyfriend, Captain Blay Farrell.

"Good teacher. Will the engineer Hokusai and the astronomer Silvio Lembo also be on the farm?

"I have said that I will take care that all five are there! The scientist replied, annoyed.

Another of the men who had remained silent, he dared to say.

"Wouldn't it be better and more useful to supplant them, Professor Hartman?

"We don't have the material; Until a new shipment we have to use ordinary means, even if they are less practical and more brutal.

"Good teacher. Gases? Bullets? Or do you prefer that ...?

"A fire" stopped the old professor.

And little by little, as an explanation for using that method, he added, to extend the orders to his men:

"I know for a fact that this little general, since he was appointed Secretary of Defense, has endowed his recreational estate with the greatest advances. Yes, gentlemen ... General Paul Quiin takes advantage of his good salary to surround himself with as many comforts as an ancient pharaoh of Egypt. Air conditioning, heating, a pool with warm water adapted to the environment, a special radio station, from there, to dispatch the most urgent matters without interrupting your rest ... Your farm is an authentic perfection! All moved by electricity.

He paused, as he accompanied his visitors, to add:

"And in a farm like this, a short circuit can be accidental. If things are done right, in a few minutes everything will burn.

"We will have to go to the farm to prepare things.

" Perfect! Do you think they can suspect you? Come on, Anderson ... Don't be naive! You are now one of the trusted men of our new Secretary of Defense. Do not forget that you are occupying the personality of Ike Anderson.

"Yes, teacher.

"Go ... I'll see that, tomorrow, the five are gathered at the farm:

"Everything will be fine," the bigger man encouraged himself.

At their comment, the elderly Professor Curt Hartman stared at them, already at the door, saying:

" I hope so! If not ... You know, folks.

Don't worry, professor. See you soon!

"We will see you at the meeting of the Galactic Central Government, when they call us to notify us ... the sad news.

When his visitors left him alone, the atomic sage crossed his office again, drew back a tapestry that covered one of the walnut walls, and pointing over his shoulder to the door, ordered another man who had remained hidden there.

"Take care of them ... Then they must die too, in that fire,

The little man did not open his lips when he said:

Yes, Professor Hartman.

* * *

It was during the 6:00 PM briefing that Blay Farrell and his wife Lise Borg learned of the accident. Apparently, a raging fire had consumed practically the entire recreational estate of the Secretary of Defense, General Paul Quiin. Unfortunately, by having as guests the cybernetic engineer Hokusai Aki and the famous astronomer Silvio Lembo both had also died.

Likewise, General Paul Quiin's aide had also been found dead, although Colonel Ike Anderson was found in the garden, along with another unidentified man. The four servants of the farm had not had time to save themselves and the experts assured that the unfortunate accident was due to a short circuit. The latest news bulletin added that later another body could be identified, which turned out to be that of Colonel Alster Holtzman, head of Prestwich Base.

Later, the informant went to other news of less importance and Blay Farrell, very affected by those losses, activated the remote control from the sofa to turn off the screen.

His pupils were riveted on his young wife's and, hoarsely, the man commented:

"Poor! Who could think of such a thing!

Lise took her husband's hands in hers and whispered:

"You were very fond of Colonel Holtzman, weren't you dear?

"He was a man of integrity. Everyone at the Base loved him.

She got up diligently, opening the closet to take out the suitcases, announcing:

"We must go back. Colonel Holtzman's widow will be comforted to see you at the funeral.

"But it's our honeymoon, Lise.

"Don't be silly. I know that deep down you prefer it that way. It would be wrong to miss funerals.

Blay Farrell did not protest again, remembering how much it had cost him to be given those days of leave to marry. When requested, Colonel Holtzman had reminded him that the time was not ripe. On the Prestwich Base were still those two extraterrestrial ships, and the orders of General Paul Quiin, as Secretary of Defense, had become even more rigid since those events: no one should enter or leave the Base, except with a special permission signed by himself. The surprising news should not be released yet, and the safest way was to isolate all personnel.

But in the secret meeting held in Colonel Holtzman's office, after assuring that they would not discuss this with anyone, the Secretary of Defense himself had given Blay Farrell those days of leave, as a kind of reward for having been the first to confront to the strange ships, of which he had disintegrated with his atomic rockets three.

As Lise continued packing, he lazily remembered that meeting in which they had also participated, as central characters. Joining the Secretary of Defense and Colonel Holtzman were the cybernetic engineer Hokusai Aki and the famous astronomer Silvio Lembo.

Now that four of the six who had attended the meeting had died, through the smoke of his cigarette Blay Farrell struggled to conjure up those scenes. He still thought he saw his boss, when Colonel Holtzman showed him General Quiin, the engineer Hokusai and the astronomer Lembo, the two robots lined up in his office:

"There you have it! "I had told them." That is all that has rained down on us from heaven. The planet that sends them is not distinguished, precisely, by its delicacy. Instead of sending us some intelligent flesh and blood, whatever they are made of, they send us those ugly machines.

However, the confrontation with the only robot that could speak was highly profitable.

And very interesting.

As an engineer in cybernetics, a specialist in science whose object is the study of control and communications in machines, Hokusai Aki soon understood that some circuit in the electronic brain of that robot had a small fault. The fact that he repeated the words tirelessly until a new emission of waves reached his receptive cells and elaborated the answer, proved this.

He wanted to repair that problem, for a better understanding with the thinking machine, and after asking permission from the Secretary of Defense, something ceremoniously approached the robot to ask:

"Can I try to fix that fault? We have also built talking robots here and I know the technique. Something is stuck until a new emission, of waves pushes the roller to elaborate another answer.

And, to the general astonishment, the robot's response was docile:

"Do it ... Do it ... Do it.

Diligently and with his dexterous hands, Hokusai Aki exposed the robot's mechanism box, and barely ten minutes later, he closed it, announcing:

"Good: this is it.

Between the smoke of his cigarette, Blay Farrell thought he saw the smile of everyone present again, when the robot answered, fully, very grateful:

"Thank you: your work has been magnificent. You are very skilled.

No less ceremonious and like a good Japanese, Hokusai Aki had bowed in the oriental style, answering:

" Very kind! But it was only one of the cohesion cables. It was mounted on the conductor that captures the Hertzian waves.

Perhaps afraid that they would engage in technical talk, General Quiin had intervened:

"What is the cohesor, friend Hokusai?

"It is a device that is used in radiotelegraphy receiving stations to report the presence of Hertzian waves, facilitating the circulation of a local current that acts on a receiving device. In this case it transmits the sounds to the nerve cells of the electronic brain, where they are registered and impel the precise answer to what has been asked.

At this, Colonel Holtzman had asked:

"Do you mean that those... those dolls can answer anything you ask them?

Blay Farrell still marveled when he remembered the reply from cyber engineer Hokusai Aki:

"They have been programmed for that, sir. The sounds produced when pronouncing a word, set in motion a roller that selects the answers. These selected signs, in turn, act on a sound drum that converts sound into voice, and this is specified in words.

"Good, but I suppose that all the sounds that we can pronounce when formulating our words, will not have an equivalent in the electronic brain that this robot has, right?

Engineer Hokusai Aki had turned to the robot, saying:

"That depends on the signs you have registered.

And without hesitation, always speaking in its metallic voice, the robot had confirmed:

"I have two billion signs, with which I can make all possible combinations.

Blay Farrell and Lise had smiled when they saw Colonel Holtzman's gaping face, an infallible sign for him, that he was perplexed.

Then, confusedly, Blay Farrell remembered everything that had been discussed there with the amazing robot. He told them that thousands of years ago it was true that their builders were sending them to Earth on an exploration mission, and that they had thus been collecting data regarding the human race, mastering all the languages and sciences that they possessed, in An attempt at an approximation impossible to make until then, because in Cygni, the planet where its builders lived, there had also been internal struggles as on Earth and, in very short periods of its long history, the planet had been ruled by the men who dreamed of that contact with other cosmic beings.

At this point, the Secretary of Defense himself had asked the robot:

"Those beings that inhabit the planet Cygni ... What are they like?

The robot had hesitated for a moment, as if it had not understood the scope of the question, until at last it answered:

"Intelligent beings. Civilized beings. Beings with a highly developed science and technique.

"No, that's not it," General Paul Quiin insisted. I mean how they are physically, externally. What do they look like?

"Beautiful. Beautiful Very developed.

Arriving here, Blay Farrell evoked the shrinking of the girl who was now his wife and continued to pack his bags, who had commented:

"Well ... It all depends on your concept of beauty. It is a very relative question.

The robot had moved the spiral joints of its neck, to address Lise Borg, stating:

"The people of Cygni are superior beings. They have defeated all the other races in their Galaxy.

Other races? "Blay Farrell himself had asked, keenly interested in what the robot was reporting to them." Do you mean that in your Galaxy there are other planets with organized, civilized life?

"Yes. But all are ruled from Cygni, except the Sosias, because they are invincible. Their very name indicates why they cannot be beaten.

Blay Farrell especially remembered this part of his conversation with the robot complex. The question asked by the wise astronomer Silvio Lembo also came to mind:

"The Sosias? Who are the Sosias?

"Ultimately, nobody knows what they really are like. The Sosias are originally from the planet Amucis in our Galaxy, but they live throughout the System, adapting to the conditions and the external appearance of the planet on which they are installed. Speaking in human terms, a Sosias can turn into a dog and live in it, an elephant, a cat, a hen ... or a man. Its outer shape changes as it suits you and where you go. That is why they are invincible, because no one can discover them. But we know that they exist and that they spread ... They always spread!

This latest information from the robot seemed to be a detailed message, which the mysterious inhabitants of Cygni intended to transmit through their robots to the inhabitants of Earth.

The noise of one of the suitcases being closed by his wife, Lise, distracted Blay Farrell from these memories, wanting to find out with his question:

"Are you really willing to give up on our honeymoon?

"After that unfortunate accident, we must do it, Blay.

"You are right. If those four men are dead, only you and I remain as eyewitnesses to everything that was discussed with Cygni's robot at that meeting. They may need us to expand on the report General Quiin presented to prominent members of the Government and ...

An idea came to his mind and he slapped his forehead, to the surprise of his wife who inquired:

"What is it, darling?

"Damn! He hadn't thought about it, until now.

"On what, Blay?

"In that all this could be the work of the Sosias! Don't you remember, Lise? The robot sent from Cygni was telling us about these beings, capable of adapting to all living conditions!

" Oh yeah! But I don't think ...

"Who knows, darling! Can we be sure that the Sosias are not already here on Earth? If so, many things would be clarified, Lise.

The woman stared at him before saying, somewhat flustered:

"It is not possible, Blay. It would be terrible!

"Of course it would be horrible! At this very moment, you yourself cannot be sure if I really am Captain Blay Farrell, or one of those strange beings who has taken my appearance. And I ... I can say the same about you!

"Shut up, please, Blay. I don't like that idea!

Neither do I, Lise. But I'm thinking ... Do you remember what Colonel Holtzman told us on the phone, when I called him to notify him that we were married much earlier than we initially thought?

"What do you mean, Blay? I don't remember anything, that should have been said to you, when after greeting him and his wife, I gave you the phone back.

"He told me what happened at the Base. Someone destroyed all twelve robots!

"Yes; now I remember that later you discussed it with me. But you told me that Colonel Holtzman had the impression that it had been an unfortunate accident and that ...

"Yes, Lise ... yet another accident! Like the one they have suffered now. Don't you see any relationship? The robots were destroyed by a short circuit, also equal to the one suffered at the estate of General Paul Quiin.

Lise stared at him, before saying:

"You're worrying me, Blay... But I don't think one has to do with the other. Other people have died on General Quiin's estate, besides him, Colonel Holtzman, his assistant, the engineer Hokusai and the astronomer Silvio Lembo. You have just heard with me that another man was also there, who has not been able to identify himself, in addition to the servants,

"Yes, but from the information of the event it appears that the general's aide and the other individual were not with them. They were found in the garden.

"If you think that someone is interested in killing all of us who could hear the information that Cygni's robot gave us, you are wrong. You and I are alive, Blay!

"True, Lise, but... why? Because even the most intimate ones were unaware that we decided to get married and go on a trip, aimlessly.

Lise Borg wanted to reassure herself and smiled, finishing packing up to head back to town. And with a certain affectionate reproach, he rejected:

"Sometimes your imagination is surprising, Blay.

CHAPTER X

As soon as they arrived in town, as they entered the apartment house, the receptionist in charge approached them saying:

"This came for you, Miss Borg. But since he didn't leave a sign or say where he was going, I ...

"It doesn't matter, Mrs. Ransky.

But when she looked at the envelope and recognized Blay Farrell's handwriting, she was puzzled. He was already entering the elevator loaded with suitcases and the woman offered him the envelope, smiling, proposing amusingly:

"You open it, darling ... Or rather, tell me by heart what you wrote to me, before I was your wife.

Blay Farrell was stumped, unable to take the envelope because his hands were full. But he protested:

"Write to you? Sorry, but I know I haven't done it for a century. These last weeks of continuous service at the Base had me very busy and ...

"Well, it's your handwriting. You do not see?

Blay put down the suitcases and took the envelope. He turned it over in his hands, and pouted with surprise as he said:

"I don't understand, Lise!

When he managed to get the written note out, his strangeness increased. There it was, written in his handwriting and his signature:

"A little change, Lise:

"I'll be waiting for you this afternoon at General Quiin's country estate. He meets us there to talk about things that interest us both. Don't miss it, darling.

"Blay."

The astronaut pilot's hand wrung the paper nervously between his fingers. Then he thought better of it and unwrinkled it, to reread the note that seemed to have been written by him.

He said nothing to the woman, but Lise understood. Her husband's voice was transformed as he asked, at last:

"What do you say to me now, Lise? Someone wrote you this note, so that you could go to the general's farm and find death there too.

"But... you didn't write it, Blay?

"Your question is absurd. Since we left the Base, we have not stopped being together, except when ...

"So, me... me... They wanted to kill me too! It is awful!

"Worse than that, Lise. It's monstrous! Whoever it is, the bastard did not know that we decided to get married and thought that you would come home, receive this note with my handwriting and go to the date ... A dirty trap!

Instinctively, the woman approached the man to say:

"I'm scared, Blay!

As soon as they got to the apartment, Lise flopped onto the couch. He hid his face in his hands and, from there, asked the man who was examining the other rooms:

"So... you really think that was murder?

"Yes darling. I believe it more and more!

"What are we going to do, Blay?

"Call the police and update them. I'll also call Lieutenant Dickson and tell him to make inquiries at Base yourself. I told you that the short circuit that destroyed the robots there had something to do with the other short circuit that happened on the general's farm.

"But ... Who could it have been?

"I don't know, honey. But the most interesting question is ... Why?

"Yeah right. All that must have a reason.

"And it must be a very important reason. Something that is related to the arrival of the spaceships from the planet Cygni.

"On the other ship, what was there, Blay?

" Nothing! And that's another mystery, Lise. Things have been rushing forward and we haven't been able to find out.

"It is not possible that there was nothing in there.

"So that's it. Cygni's talking robot told us that the other ship was also manned by robots. Colonel Holtzman sent a group of technicians to come after them. I think the door opened, it lit up and there is the surprising thing ... There was no one inside!

"Who could man it, then?

" And what I know? The technicians entered it and came out saying that the ship was empty.

"Maybe driven by a remote control, from Cygni?

"Impossible, Lise! As an astronomer and from the data and distances that the robot gave us, Professor Lembo calculated that this planet is about twenty thousand light-years from our Solar System. He deduced that the Sun or the star that warms that remote world, must be in the Constellation of Libra. And it is completely inconceivable to suppose that a ship can be directed, by remote control, at such a great distance.

"Twenty thousand light-years away! "Repeated the woman." How is it possible that those ships from Cygni got here?

"Distances do not exist for them, because the centrifugal force that moves them multiplies by twenty or thirty thousand the speed of light. Their total spherical shape makes them glide through hyperspace with the smoothness of an atom. But even so, the robot told us, it takes many years to reach us and that is the problem that its builders, the inhabitants of Cygni, cannot solve. If they came themselves, instead of sending their robots to try to establish contact with us, they would arrive very old. Or dead!

The silence that followed Blay Farrell's explanation was broken after a few minutes of reflection, when the woman said:

"But, Blay... I'm thinking that something else follows from what you said.

"The what, Lise?

"That those ... those Sosias that you fear, are already here, among us, they could not arrive either. The distance is enormous and they would not endure such a journey.

"And who tells us that, in addition to being able to adapt to any form of life or outward appearance, they do not also have the power to live long, but much more than us or the inhabitants of Cygni?

"You mean that they can be immortal beings?

"I don't know, Lise. I have the feeling that we are rambling. And God grant it to be so!

He picked up the intercom to contact the police, and at that moment the doorbell rang. Lise got up wearily to go, but her husband hung up the phone, exclaiming:

"No, Lise! Don't open yourself!

The two of them were very close together in the corridor and they called again. They looked at each other uneasily and she wanted to calm down, thinking:

"It will be the receptionist. Mrs. Ransky must have forgotten to tell me something.

"Yes, Lise... Open up, but I'll be in that room, watching. I do not want to scare you with my precautions and thoughts, but they do not hurt, in view of everything that happens. Okay, honey?

"You command, my love.

Minutes later, the frank and friendly smile of Lieutenant Pat Summer greeted the owner of the house:

"How are you, Lise?

Lise Borg was still a bit hesitant; worried about everything she had been talking about with her husband. This hesitation was taken advantage of by the young pilot, to inquire:

"May I come in, miss? Ah, sorry! I meant Mrs. Farrell.

Upon entering, the jovial visitor inquired, looking around:

"Isn't Blay there?

"Well ... now it's coming. Won't you have a drink, Pat?

"No, nothing. Thanks, Lise.

Then, almost without transition and staring at him, in a somewhat strange way the visitor inquired:

"Why didn't you go to General Quiin's estate?

Lise Borg stood there, standing before him, galvanized. In front of him was young pilot Pat Summer, one of Blay Farrell's best teammates. But why was he asking that question? What did he know about the note that the receptionist had given them as soon as they entered the building?

The woman wanted to buy time to respond and get out of her astonishment and, in turn, inquired:

"What did you say, Pat?

There were no more friendly or kind intonations in the young pilot's voice, saying:

"Why didn't you go to General Quiin's estate? Blay would quote you there. Wasn't it, Lise?

She also changed her intonation, staring at him, as she replied:

"These are things you don't care about, Pat.

" You're wrong! We care a lot about all this ...

" U.S? Who are you talking about, Pat?

"It is irrelevant ... Only now things will have to happen differently.

Lise Borg felt her legs shake. But knowing that Blay was listening to them from the next room encouraged her, finding the courage to invite him again:

Sit down, Pat. So you can explain that strange attitude to me. You were always a kind and polite boy and now ...

"You don't know how I always was!

His scornful exclamation was restrained by the weapon in his left hand, speaking again as he indicated the sofa with his right:

"Sit there, dear Lise... I'm going to give you an injection.

Lise Borg was almost on the verge of screaming, calling for her husband. But he quickly calculated that if Blay did not come, it was for something, and summoned all the serenity he had to whisper weakly:

"What's that about, Pat? No ... I don't understand!

Pat Summer smiled, seeing the frightened woman tremble before him. He kept pointing the gun in his left hand at her, while with his right, digging into the bottom of his uniform pocket, he kept looking for something he was trying to pull out.

At last he put a syringe and a tube that seemed to contain a hypodermic needle on the table, shook a small container, before the blue eyes of his victim, and announced:

"Fear not, dear Lise... It is painless and you will sleep... You will sleep forever!

" Oh my God! Are you ... are you going to kill me, Pat? But why?

"Even if I try to explain my reasons to you, you won't understand them, Lise. Trust me!

"But you want to murder me! As you did with General Quiin and his guests!

Pat Summer seemed to smile grotesquely, exclaiming:

" Wow! So you think General Quiin and his guests didn't accidentally die, do you, Lise? Sorry, but ... You have to cease to exist!

Nerves taut, with his regulation weapon in hand, Blay Farrell listened to all this and struggled not to intervene, eager to learn more; learn more about the secret behind all that.

But the threatened woman was Lise, his wife, being idolized above all things and he was no longer able to think more than that.

So he walked steadily down the corridor and yelled, pointing at the scoundrel:

"Drop the gun, Pat! Let go of her, or for God's sake I'm leaving you dry!

Pat Summer didn't obey. He gave a cry of a cornered beast as he felt deceived and surprised, turning in tandem on his heel to activate his index finger. The bullet passed within inches of Blay Farrell's shoulder as he dropped to the ground and fired in turn.

And his shot was fatal.

Pat Summer bent over like a dry branch broken off by a hurricane, dragging the small table in his fall where he had deposited the syringe and the tube with the hypodermic needle.

And then something totally unexpected and surprising happened.

The small vial that Pat Summer had waved before Lise's eyes broke as it hit the ground. A dense cloud of bluish smoke erupted, the liquid began to grow and grow, as if in contact with the air it multiplied itself, concentrating on a large stain that began to spread throughout the carpet.

Terrified, her nerves broken, Lise Borg ran to take refuge in the arms of her husband, who did not take his eyes off that red, liquid and slimy stain, which seemed to have a life of its own and was advancing towards Pat Summer's body.

When the red stain reached the dead man's hand, it crawled up his fingers, and as it did so, as it impregnated him, the flesh thinned out to become, in turn, more red liquid that grew and grew steadily.

" It is awful! The woman screamed, terrified,

"Yes, Lise... Horrible, but at the same time... Amazing!

It was, because, before his eyes, barely ten feet away, the red liquid continued to permeate the body of what was pilot Pat Summer, and as it did so, the corpse disappeared, bubbling as if it were boiling.

Unable to witness the horrible spectacle that, at the same time, attracted them like a powerful magnet, when the red liquid continued to rise and had already washed up to the waist from Pat Summer's body, the woman fainted.

Blay Farrell felt her gravitate with all her weight, in his arms, and he knew he must carry her away. Loaded with it, he dodged the bloody mass that seemed to continue boiling on the floor as best he could, reaching the exit to advance down the corridor.

CHAPTER XI

When he returned to Lise Borg's apartment, Blay Farrell couldn't believe his eyes. He kept looking at the ground, and once more repeated to Inspector Hoffenblad:

"I tell you that everything happened here before our sight!

Lewis Hoffenblad, a man accustomed to dealing with the most unusual cases, in his long professional career, consulted a notebook containing the first statements of Captain Blay Farrell and calmly said:

"Let's go in parts, Captain. Are you still insisting that the man who came to see you was Lieutenant Pat Summer?

"How can I not insist, Inspector? Both my wife and I knew him perfectly. He was stationed, too, at Prestwich Base!

The policeman showed himself patience and asked again:

"Why do you say we met and were, Captain Farrell? Do you think Lieutenant Pat Summer no longer exists?

" Well of course! We saw him disappear, little by little, before our eyes, Inspector!

Lewis Hoffenblad looked at his two uniformed officers for a moment, then replied:

"Dice disappeared eaten by the red liquid that gushed out of the small vial in his hand. It is not like this?

"You don't believe me, do you, Inspector?

"Well, Captain... The truth is that here there is no trace of all that you say happened before your very eyes!

"Not just before mine, but also before my wife's.

"The bad thing is that his wife cannot be questioned now. He's still in the hospital, unconscious.

"When he recovers, he will be able to repeat my words. And he will tell you about the carpet, which has also disappeared!

" Already...! In conjunction with the corpse, the vial with the mysterious red liquid, the table, the syringe, the hypodermic needle ... And everything! Right, Captain?

Blay Farrell was beginning to find himself annoyed, even with himself. It all seemed absurd, but he knew it had been true.

Or did he have to admit he was crazy, as the cops were surely beginning to think?

He was silent, his eyes always fixed on the floor, where he had seen the red liquid run on the carpet. And finding no sign, no trace of everything that had happened, already tired, he limited himself to saying:

"Good, inspector. You can think what you want, but I confirm myself in my statement. And why the hell would I call you, if none of all that I told you happened here?

"That is a question I wish I could answer, Captain Farrell. You are a common man, capable of hallucinations.

"It was not a hallucination!

Calm down, captain. Calm down! We are not implying that he is crazy or lied to us. It just happens that we have a hard time believing everything he has told us.

"It's natural. These are not things that happen normally, inspector.

"How long were you out of this room?

"I don't know, Inspector. I can't pin it down. When my wife fainted at that horrible sight, I thought it appropriate to take her to the apartment of her neighbor, Mrs. Hons, to better serve her there, with her help.

"Did you use Mrs. Hons's phone to call us, Captain?

"Yes, I did, once I was sure that an ambulance would come from the hospital.

"Let's see ... All of that could have taken about twelve or fifteen minutes. It is not like this?

"Exactly about twenty, Inspector. I know it well, because I kept looking at the clock. Then, in the ambulance, I accompanied my wife to the hospital and begged Mrs. Hons to tell you that she would be there, if you arrived before I returned.

One of the uniformed officers made a gesture to interrupt what his boss was about to reply:

"Say, Jeff" encouraged the inspector.

"We were in the hospital for about fifteen minutes, listening" he interrupted. " Well, listening to everything the captain told us.

"Thanks, Jeff, twenty minutes and fifteen is thirty-five, added to about ten that it took us to get here and another seven to locate you at the hospital, it adds up to fifty-two minutes ... Let's put an hour, counting what we have long to get back here, to this room.

"In that time, someone has been able to be here and make the carpet and everything else disappear.

Blay Farrell's calculation didn't seem far-fetched, but the inspector insisted:

"And what about the surprising fact that a good friend knocked on that door with the intention of murdering his wife? What motives could he have?

"Excuse me, Inspector. There are some things I haven't told you yet.

Inspector Lewis Hoffenblad looked at him, between stern and amused, as he encouraged him:

"Go ahead, captain! What are you waiting for?

"The thing is ... These are things that are going to surprise you even more.

" More...? I assure you that after what you have told us, there will be few things that can surprise us, friend.

"Well, well... there it goes!

Blay Farrell took a deep breath, looked at the three men one by one, and finally decided:

"I think Lieutenant Pat Summer was not human... I mean, a being like us.

The question sprouted simultaneously from the mouths of the three policemen:

"How do you say, captain?

"You have already heard it. Pat Summer was not a human being. He hadn't been born on Earth ... Or, at least, if he had been born here, lately it wasn't him ... Well, I mean another being lived inside him, using his body to ...

"Stop, Captain Farrell! "The inspector stopped, annoyed". I think we've heard you enough by now and that you too should have stayed in the hospital.

He turned to one of his agents and added, this time more forcefully:

"Call for an ambulance, Jeff. And let them come with the straitjacket!

Blay Farrell bounced up and took a few steps away from the three policemen. He stood behind the back of the long sofa, putting that weak barrier between him and them, rejecting:

"I repeat that I am not crazy! You have to listen to me! Things have happened lately that you and most of the people are unaware of! Haven't they heard of UFOs, Flying Saucers?

The inspector smiled, saying:

"Yes, sure ... But you are like a goat!

And when he saw that Blay Farrell moved, showing that he was not willing to have their hands laid on him, he ordered his men again:

"At the door, Jeff. This guy must not leave here! You call Central, Guy.

"At your service, Inspector.

Blay Farrell saw the agent pick up the phone and again yelled:

" Not! Wait! They are things that should not transcend! I myself had orders not to divulge them! They are only known to some members of the Central Galactic Government! Why do you think that all the air bases on Earth are on alert, without letting their personnel leave?

He saw that the inspector was staring at him, but gesturing to Agent Guy not to dial on the phone. That encouraged Blay, when he saw that he was getting ready to listen again, and he blurted out:

"Yes, Inspector ... Lately we have been in contact with inhabitants of other worlds.

Inspector Lewis Hoffenblad asked pointedly:

"Repeat that, Captain Farrell.

"There are two alien ships at Prestwich Base, Inspector. I know that very few people are aware of this amazing event, apart from the personnel stationed there, but what I am telling you is the truth.

"Did you say two alien ships, Captain?

"Two UFOs, or two Flying Saucers, Inspector, whatever you want to call them. They arrived manned by robots, sent to us by the inhabitants of the planet Cygni, who according to the astronomer Lembo ...

" One moment! Are you referring to Professor Silvio Lembo who died on General Paul Quiin's estate, in that unfortunate accident?

"Yes, inspector. But that fire was not an accident. It was murder!

" How...?

"They will remember the people who died there. They, except for the servants and General Quiin's assistant, along with an unidentified man, who was accompanying him, were present at the conversation they had with the robot and ...

The inspector again exchanged silent glances with his two assistants, and more incredulously asked again:

"You want us to believe that someone was talking to robots?

"Yes. Colonel Holtzman, Engineer Hokusai Aki, Astronomer Lembo, my wife, and myself.

Blay Farrell noticed that the smile on the lips of the two agents was accentuated, looking at their boss with great amusement. That's why he stopped:

"I know you will also find it very strange, but it was like that. Together we prepared the report for the Secretary of Defense, General Quiin.

Lewis Hoffenblad drummed his fingers on the back of the sofa that kept separating them from the man who was telling them all this with the utmost seriousness, succeeding only in whispering:

"Well, well, well ... It's a nice story, Captain Farrell. But there are some things that don't fit.

"For example, Inspector?

"First: if you say that no one can get out of Prestwich Base, what the hell are you doing outside of it?

"The same Secretary of Defense gave me permission. I was going to marry Miss Lise Borg. That has saved us!

"How do you say?

"That if the two had not left the Base with an unknown destination, on our honeymoon, now surely we would already be dead. I have proof of what I say, Inspector!

"What evidence?

"My wife received a letter, inviting her to General Quiin's farm, which she could not open because she was absent on that trip.

Who wrote that invitation letter?

"We ignore it. But the lyrics are forged. It's mine!

" How?

"That's right, Inspector. The killer hoped that, upon receiving my note, Lise would come to the farm, so that she would die there, too.

"Why do you think they wanted to kill her?

"For the same reason that General Quiin and the others have been assassinated. Because of information transmitted by the robot from Cygni!

What kind of information?

"Among other things, he told us about the Sosias.

"The Partners, Captain? Believe me, we understand you less and less. I try to listen to him without losing patience, but ...

"And I understand that all this may seem very strange to you, when not, the talk of a madman, of a madman. But I assure you that it is all true! You can check later, inspector.

"All right, captain. What did he say about those Sosias?

"Apparently, they are strange beings capable of adapting to other kinds of life, adopting a thousand forms, the one that suits them best. Lieutenant Pat Summer was one of them!

"How do you know?

"Because my wife and I watched him disappear, turning his body into that horrible compact and viscous liquid. Otherwise, I don't understand how, being our longtime friend, he came here to kill Lise.

"I assure you, my head is spinning, Captain. But if I do not misunderstand, you mean that these beings ... those Sosias, can live inside any person, they adopt their appearance. It is not like this?

"I don't know how they get it, but it must be like that. I repeat that the robot told us about them too.

Inspector Lewis Hoffenblad had an idea:

"The best thing is to move to Prestwich Base and have me see those ships myself and talk to the robot. Don't you think, Captain?

Blay Farrell didn't answer. He wasn't quite sure if they would let them in. At least the orders to keep those secrets were very specific. He himself doubted how right he had been to talk about all this, despite his circumstances.

Of course they had tried to assassinate his wife and he was almost certain that General Quiin and his guests had not been the victims of an accident, but of a mysterious conspiracy. He thought that, later, he would justify himself to his bosses and so he encouraged:

"We can go to Base, Inspector. Whenever you want.

CHAPTER XII

As they were getting down in the elevator, when the doors opened, two nurses from the Central Hospital appeared before them, accompanied by Professor Curt Hartman. And the atomic sage indicated, addressing the inspector:

"This man must be immediately hospitalized!

Blay Farrell was petrified, crushing everyone as if looking for an answer. The inspector's gaze was so eloquent that he even smiled at him, commenting:

"I already said I was crazy, friend! All that you have told us is fantastic.

Without giving himself time to defend himself, Professor Curt Hartman began to justify:

"Many times, in space flight, astronauts get unbalanced and upset. But with proper medical treatment, they soon recover and ...

It was too much!

Blay Farrell jumped back, yelling at everyone:

"Noses! I am perfectly fine! And I don't know why you say that, Professor Hartman!

"Come on, come on, Blay! Don't be a child. You know you need care!

" Me?

"You, my friend, you. Otherwise, he would not have attacked his wife.

"I attack Lise? "He repeated." Here, the one who is crazy is you!

Ignoring their protests, in a calm and calm tone, the prestigious atomic sage commented, addressing the inspector and his two agents:

"Excuse me, but this man must be admitted immediately. If he has something pending with you, in a few hours you will be able to see him at the Central Hospital. But now...

The silent signal he made to the two nurses who accompanied him once again put Blay Farrell on the offensive, who, backing down the corridor, insisted:

"Why do you insist on wanting to take me to the hospital?

"Calm down, Blay, you have your wife there and besides, you need to be treated and... We do everything for your good!

Curt Hartman made a studied pause and again looking at the cops, clarified:

"I don't know what he may have told you, Inspector. But I assure you that this man's wife was very scared when she saw him excited, telling her very strange things. He began to speak of beings from other planets, of a red liquid ... What do I know of how many more nonsense! She didn't believe him and that's when he attacked her.

" He is lying! I didn't attack Lise!

But Inspector Lewis Hoffenblad had heard enough and decided, turning to his men when he saw that Blay Farrell was about to flee:

"To him, boys!

Blay Farrell kept backing away to get defensive, but moments later he had to fight these men, desperately. And he would have beaten them if the elderly Professor Curt Hartman, slyly standing behind him, had not hit him on the head and knocked him out of his mind.

* * *

In the straitjacket, nearly preventing all movement, Blay Farrell felt helpless. He was lying on a bed and realized, when he came to, that the walls of that room were padded. To his right was a small table and, on it, several bottles.

There was also a syringe and a hypodermic needle, to give injections.

But what most alarmed him was the discovery of a small vial filled with a red liquid that looked like plasma.

Blood!

It alarmed him because, without any doubt, he identified him with the one he had briefly seen in the murderous hands of Lieutenant Pat Summer, when he went to Lise's apartment to murder the girl. He shifted on the bed and raised his head as far as he could, shouting:

" Nurse! To me! To me!

Despite the straitjacket that imprisoned him, he managed to get up, and then his eyes revealed a familiar face. It was Professor Curt Hartman smiling at him from the back of the room.

The two men glared at each other, Blay Farrell with hatred and the atomic sage with irony and mockery.

I was smiling at him ...

Blay Farrell recalled, and when the old man walked up to him, he furiously inquired:

"What the hell are you doing here and why did you insist that they put me in the hospital?

"I will accommodate all your questions, Blay. With great pleasure!

"I start by telling me why they put me here.

"You are going to undergo a very... special treatment, my friend.

"What do you gain by pretending that I am crazy?

Before answering, the old man glanced furtively at the door to the room, as if to make sure it was still closed. Then, his eyes went to the table to fixate on the vial with the red liquid, while his well-groomed hands manipulated the syringe, arming it with the hypodermic needle.

And he spoke with pause:

"I have brought you here, because it suits you, friend Blay. You will be very well soon!

"What are you going to inject me? What's that? "Inquired the man, trapped in those clothes that did not allow him to defend himself.

The four pupils were drilling again and the old man put great emphasis, when he whispered:

"I'm going to inject Life Sap into him, Blay! Sap of a life that will amaze you!

Some kind of light flashed in Blay Farrell's brain, forcing him to say:

"Professor Hartman, you ... You are one of yours! Truth? It's one of those Sosias!

"Yes, my friend ... And in this hospital there are several like us.

"And what is he going to inject me with? Is ... is this how they transform? The way Pat Summer wanted to do with my wife?

"I see you are still so smart, Blay. That's how it is!

And after speaking, sitting on the edge of the bed and showing him the small vial of red liquid, he expanded, with an insinuating voice:

"You'll see how sweet it is! Here is the vital fluid of a Sosia! You have traveled through space for many years, my friend! It didn't come meant for you, but it complicated things and ... You have to be one of us!

Helpless in those clothes, Blay Farrell was annoyed by that tutelage and everything that Professor Hartman was doing. He looked at him as if hypnotized when he saw him load the syringe with that red liquid and he cried out desperately:

" Not! Not me! HELP!

"Don't be a kid, Blay. No one can hear you. This room is built soundproof. So that crazy people like you don't bother!

" I'm not crazy! You made them think so!

"It was accurate... You talked too much about everything the robot said. Nobody on Earth ... Nobody, Blay !, must know that there are beings on other worlds who can take on an outward appearance. That would alarm them, and they would be on their guard!

Struggling uselessly inside those clothes that held him to the bed, he found the courage to say, seeing that the needle was already approaching his arm:

Why do you want to live here on Earth? Are you not well in your world?

"Yes very good! But we aspire to dominate the entire Universe. And we are getting it! We do not have weapons as powerful as you or the intelligent inhabitants of the planet Cygni ... But we use their fast ships to reach all the planets! Without knowing it, they serve us themselves ... And many of Cygni's inhabitants are already ours!

"And here, on Earth?

"Also... We are already millions, Blay! Millions!

" Not! I deny that!

"You can deny it, Blay. But it's true! Myself, who everyone still believes Professor Curt Hartman ... Ha ha ha!

That almost hysterical laugh chilled the blood of Blay Farrell, who was deeply impressed by everything he heard.

How was all this possible?

"Easy, Blay. Do not worry! Apparently, you will still be Blay Farrell, the excellent pilot who recently married Lise Borg. You will not change anything at all! But human blood will no longer run through your veins, as through mine already runs that of another being who came here in these little bottles.

"I will never give up my human condition! Protested, helplessly, Blay Farrell.

"You can't help it.

"But I... I will die! He's going to kill me! He's going to murder me!

"You reason wrong, Blay ... You will die, but another being will live in your body.

"A monstrous being! Since when are they coming to Earth?

"Since the inhabitants of Cygni arrived here with their ships. It's been a long time!

Blay Farrell remembered. And more than his fear, could his curiosity, saying:

"Are they, those robots that send us from Cygni, the ones that bring you, without knowing it?

"Yes, my friend. I told you before! They are machines that, no matter how sophisticated they are, it is easy to fool them. In Cygni we have many of our own, infiltrators. They are the ones who place the vials with the vital sap. When we get here we just have to inject it into a human body and ...

Blay knew that he, as a human body, was going to die. He knew that his physical envelope would be used for one of those strange beings to live in him. From that, he would collaborate in his work of penetration of the race of the Sosias.

How many human wraps already served like this? What high positions did they hold? What key sites had they infiltrated?

What was his real power on Earth?

What is his last end ...?

He didn't have time to answer as many questions as they were being asked in his tortured mind. But the remaining minutes of his life, still the real Blay Farrell, he would use to fight like a human being. To fight as befits a child of Earth.

He was helpless, imprisoned in that suit. But he had intelligence left and he would use it.

At least to buy time.

"Tell me something, professor ... Why didn't you find other robots, manning the other ship?

"They found them, Blay! But Colonel Holtzman sent Lieutenant Pat Summer, unaware that he was already one of us. He was in charge of injecting the men who accompanied him ...! And the transplantation was done! Precisely the shipments, arrived in that ship. When they came out, they were all ours. Do you understand now?

"And what happened to the one who was occupying Pat Summer's body? I saw him disappear into my wife's apartment. His body turned into red liquid, when he came into contact with the one that was poured from the vial he was carrying.

"That is our death, Blay! If the Sap of Life is poured out before entering the body of another being, it spreads, spreads, cooks, boils and, finally, is consumed. It needs the wrapping of another body, to continue living!

"Who changed the stained carpet? "He wanted to know.

" U.S! You were very busy with your wife's fainting.

Blay saw those hands approaching his brave to stab him with the needle and shouted:

"You will never achieve your ends! NEVER!

" You're wrong! We are not powerful like you, but no one has been able, until now, to identify us. We have the ability to adopt a thousand forms, and thus we can live on all planets. In different worlds! And our greatest power is that.

"Now I understand why you murdered General Quiin and his guests. Because the robot told us about the Members. Yours!

"Yes ... In Cygni they already know of our existence. But without being unable to identify us! All his marvelous and advanced science, nothing can against us.

He paused and added:

"For example, who would suspect that you are not still Blay Farrell, even though, in reality, you are not? If I hadn't told you, would you have suspected that I was not Professor Curt Hartman? You will leave here cured of your visions and attacks of madness. You will return to service at the Prestwich Base, but since you will already be a Sosia, one of us ... you will serve us from there!

"Dirty move! It's an invasion of worms!

"No, Blay: say rather that it is a very clever invasion. The day will come when all the key positions will be in our hands and then ...

"What will happen then, monster? Cried Blay, helplessly.

He did not get an answer, because that being was leaning towards the man's arm again, ready to give him the injection.

Blay Farrell could do nothing and closed his eyes.

He pretended to refuse to believe that he, his entire body, would soon be the shelter for a strange being from another planet.

But it would be like this ...

CHAPTER XIII

The friendly hand of Inspector Lewis Hoffenblad was extended to the man before him, congratulating him:

"You were very brave, Blay.

The young pilot smiled too, but it was to reject:

"Don't believe it... It was terrible! I felt that...

"I understand what he would feel at times like this, but he had the guts to argue with the fake professor Curt Hartman and stuff ... That gave us a lot of clues!

"The truth, Inspector. I was unaware that they had installed microphones in that room to record everything that was spoken there.

"All the more reason for me to congratulate you, Blay. I did it because, in a way, even though I also thought you were crazy, because of everything you told us, I was intrigued by Professor Hartman's interest in admitting you to the hospital and ...

He made a gesture with his hands and, as if to excuse himself, said:

"You know, Blay! Cops are like that! We suspect, as a rule, of everything!

"Are they all being located? "The young pilot wanted to know.

" Oh yeah!

"Is it very difficult to get it?

" Unlike! All it takes is a blood test. This is how they are hunted!

For a minute, the two friends were silent, until Captain Farrell wanted to specify:

"How many so far, Inspector?

"Well, about six million ... Of course, scattered everywhere.

"Among our officers, too?

"Also. They were the favorites, for them. But great caution has been used. Districts have been cordoned off, health teams have turned up unexpectedly and ... Let's get to work! Not one can escape: from now on it will be a matter of sewing and singing.

Blay Farrell remembered again and almost shivered as he said:

"One more minute to enter that room ... And I am not me, at this hour, Inspector!

"We were prepared. I never would have let you get injected, Blay. Everything we had heard was enough.

It was difficult to get away from this hot topic, but the policeman thought it wise to ask:

" And his wife?

"It is all right: the poor thing has not come to know that she too was chosen to be injected.

"I'm glad: you both have the right to the happiness that now awaits you.

Blay Farrell smiled, but announced:

"A lot of work awaits us too, Lewis. We are among those who have to start the Great Project.

"You mean attempting the journey to the planet Cygni?

"That's.

" Good adventure! That must be a long way off.

"True, but... I'll tell you, Lewis. The Earth owes its existence to the beings that populate that world. They conditioned the electronic brains in their robots, to warn us of the existence of the Sosias. Otherwise ... how would we have found out?

"Yes, Blay, but ... How do you get there?

"Don't your ships get here?

"Certain. But driven by robots!

"We can do the same. The case is to get in touch. On the other hand, by copying the mechanisms of their spaceships we will advance a lot. For centuries, they have been sending their UFOs, making a titanic effort. Now it's our turn.

The policeman smiled again when he said, very satisfied:

"The truth is that we have won the battle against those Sosias.

"Certain; here on Earth they have been located and defeated, but the fight must go on, my friend. You already know that they can survive in whatever body they use! That is why we are interested in entering into constant communication with the inhabitants of Cygni. Between them and us, anywhere in the Universe where they are located ... They will be fought!

"I trust the human race, Blay. And I trust so much because, as long as there are men like you, of your mettle and courage ... The Earth will remain the same!

Thank you Lewis.

* * *

The two were walking hand in hand under a starry night, when looking up at the black sky and staring at one of the distant luminous points, the woman whispered:

"Do you think Cygni will get our message, darling?

Blay Farrell also stared into infinity, answering:

"Sure, Lise. And from now on the Universe will get smaller!

"What if we don't get it?

"We will keep trying!

They continued walking in silence, until again the woman broke it by saying, following the course of her thoughts:

"Sometimes I wonder why, throughout its long history, the human race has always had to fight.

"Ask yourself another question, honey.

"Which one, Blay?"

"Wouldn't the intelligence and the human spirit go dormant, if it were not so?

The woman reflected, before admitting:

"Yes I think so.

"The great goals are achieved by working and overcoming all obstacles. And just as the crops are better once the land has been cleared of the tares, future conquests of space will be more fruitful and better as intelligent beings defeat the Sosias or the inhabitants of other distant planets, who seek to interrupt this constant evolution towards higher goals.

Lise looked at her husband, interrupted her march to hug him and rest her head on his male chest, whispering:

"And I am very proud of you, Blay. I am, because you are one of those chosen ones!

He kissed her.

And perhaps the stars, from their remote distances, for an instant shone brighter in the harmony of the Universe.

END

www.ingramcontent.com/pod-product-compliance
Lightning Source LLC
Chambersburg PA
CBHW021006180726
47993CB00017B/1014